HIS PROMISE

BY

ANGEL RAYNE

SYNOPSIS

In my world, good guys don't exist. There are only villains, monsters, and me. I'm the thing the monsters fear.

Every mafia boss needs a guy who'll fight dirty and do whatever is asked of him, no matter how brutal.

I'm that guy.

Morally gray doesn't begin to describe me. I feel nothing. Love no one. And that's how I like it.

Until *her*.

Serafina Cordero is the runaway mafia princess I've been ordered to find and return to her sadistic father. He wants to force her into an arranged marriage. I shouldn't care.

But I do.

Because the moment I laid eyes on her, I *knew* she would be mine. It doesn't matter that it's forbidden, or that she's a virgin as innocent as I am dark and depraved.

For once in my life, I'm not following orders. I'm keeping
Sera.

And if anyone tries to take her from me, I can promise
them one thing.

They won't live long enough to regret it...

PROLOGUE

E nzo

Blood spattered the walls of our bedroom, transforming our loving home into something I normally kept far, far away from those who lived here. The two people who meant more to me than anyone in this fucked up world.

I stood frozen—numb—in the center of the room as my eyes traveled over the walls and bed. The photo on the nightstand of the two of us on our honeymoon smiling into the camera like the stupid, lovesick kids we were, dripped with blood. A piece of flesh hung on the corner, clinging to the wood in a desperate attempt to stay where it was before it finally succumbed to gravity and landed in the small pool of blood beneath it with a plop. The entire scene was like something out of a nightmare. The faces in the photo completely unrecognizable now.

My fingers went lax, and the gun slid from my hand to land on the hardwood floor with a loud thud. Silent tears ran down my face. "Why did you make me do this, Ale? Why?" I asked her. "WHY??"

My wife stared back at me with dark eyes that were vacant of the life that had once lit them from within. A life full of love and laughter. A life we had made together.

I refused to look below her neck, not wanting to see what I had done. I hadn't shot her in the face or head. I couldn't bring myself to do it, even though it would've been a quicker death. Because if I had, that would be the last image I had of my wife. That was the way I would always remember her. "Alessandra..." I whispered her name, afraid that, wherever she was, she would hear me and see what I'd done. Would she haunt me now? Destroy our beautiful home in her ethereal rage? The home I'd helped build with my bare hands?

My legs suddenly gave out, and I fell to my knees beside the gun, then forward onto my hands. Crawling across the floor, I somehow made my way over to her, slipping and sliding through the blood that trailed across the floor. I could barely see as an excruciating pain ripped open my chest, laying my heart bare, and tears streamed down my face. But somehow, I managed to find her hand. It lay limp and cold on the floor, and I picked it up and held it to my chest with both of mine, trying in vain to keep it warm.

Was she holding our son right now? Would she tell him how much I love him? How much I miss him?

Elliot had been gone for nearly a year, but I could still see his intelligent brown eyes. Still hear his giggles as I walked through the house when I got home, searching for my family, only to find them in some far corner of the house playing in whatever imaginary world they were visiting that day. He'd only lived four precious years before he was taken from us by a stray bullet. A bullet that had been meant for me.

After it happened, I'd gone a little bit mad for a while.

For Ale, the madness had never left.

I'd tried to keep her safe. To keep her in the background, where I'd hoped Luigi, the boss of the Italian mafia in Austin, would forget she even existed. I told her over and over that our son's death was nothing but an accident, and there wasn't anything that could've been done. But she wouldn't fucking listen to me. She was a mother who'd lost her child, and she wanted revenge against the man responsible. For her, that man wasn't the gunman, but Luigi, the one who'd groomed me since I was a child to join this life of crime.

We were young when we met, Alessandra and I. Teenagers. Way too young to fall in love and get married, even though we'd waited until she was finished with school. By that time, I'd already held my position as one of Luigi's top soldiers for two years. One of only two people he trusted with his youngest son.

Alessandra wasn't from our world. She hated the fact that I was involved with the mafia and was always telling me to get out and find a respectable job. However, this life she hated so much was the only one I knew. What else was I supposed to do? I never went to college. Never learned a trade. As a member of La Cosa Nostra, I could provide well for her and any children we might have. She'd always have a good home. She wouldn't have to work unless she wanted to. And she'd have the other wives to keep her company.

But she wanted nothing to do with any of it. And when Elliot had died, she'd blamed me. Blamed the family. Especially Luigi. As the boss, she believed he should've protected us. And she was right. However, if I'd gone after him, I only would've been signing my own death warrant. I would've left her completely alone in this world that would never accept her but would never allow her to be free. Because even with me gone, she would never be allowed to escape. I was smart enough to know this.

Alessandra hadn't cared.

She'd gotten out of control. First attacking him with her bare fists at the funeral, and then driving to his house with one of my guns. And it had only gotten worse from there.

Before I knew it, she was snooping around on my computer and phone, trying to find the right time and place to get to him. This she admitted openly to me, throwing it in my face that she'd been able to get into everything so easily, and eventually I had no choice but to tell Luigi so he could take precautions. I told him she was grieving as any mother would, and that over time she would grow to accept our son's death. He listened and was sympathetic, but he couldn't take the chance that she would somehow get through his men. However, to show his appreciation of my loyalty, or maybe to test it further, he told me I could be the one to take her out. Before she did something really stupid and got someone else killed or brought the FBI down on our heads.

Horrified that he'd even suggest such a thing, I tried to reassure him that I would make sure she never got anywhere near him. I offered to send her away. Swore to talk sense into her. I told him she was still mourning our son, that she just needed time. But all of my pleading fell on deaf ears. Even Luca, his own son and one of my best friends, couldn't talk him out of his decision. If I didn't do it, someone else would.

I went home that night and made love to my wife for hours, bringing her to orgasm over and over until she was sobbing and reaching for me. Only then did I take my own pleasure in her sweet body, fucking her like it was the last time I would ever be able to do so.

And then I got up from the bed, retrieved my gun from the top of the dresser, and I shot her in the center of her chest as she slept.

"You were mine," I told her as I held her hand in the ever-growing puddle of blood soaking my bare skin. "MINE. Why wouldn't you stop, Ale? Why couldn't you let it go?" I sniffed and started rubbing her arm. She was growing so cold and pale. "*Caro*, this was a war that would have no winner. It was a war we couldn't win. Why couldn't you see that? Why wouldn't you believe me? Even if I'd chosen you, we wouldn't have gotten away. We would both be dead now."

Perhaps that would be better, I thought as I pulled my wife's body up onto my lap. The sobs I couldn't hold back anymore wracked through me as I hunched over her as though I could protect her in death like I couldn't in life.

Three days later, dressed in my finest black Armani suit, I stood beside her open grave and watched as they lowered her body into the ground beside our son's. The funeral had been expedited. Luigi wanted this "mess" forgotten as soon as possible.

"At least she didn't suffer," Luca told me. "She didn't even know it was coming. It was better this way."

Yes, I knew this to be true. Luigi wasn't known to be a compassionate man, and he didn't appreciate the fact that I was unable to keep my wife under control. If I had refused to carry out his orders, he would've sent his men after her. And as much as it hurt me to do it myself, I couldn't stand the thought of another man's hands on her. Of someone else hurting her. And they would've hurt her in ways I couldn't even imagine. She'd threatened the boss's life. There was no other way this could've ended.

Luca's next words interrupted my grief. "Thank you."

"For what?" I asked him.

"For staying with me," he said. "I need you, Enzo. I'm glad you made the right decision."

"I'm not so sure that I did," I told him quietly as I watched people dressed in mourning clothes throw handfuls of dirt on Alessandra's coffin and begin to wander off. Back to their lives. Where they would tell each other what a shame it was that it had come to this as they went about their business like nothing had happened. Like my heart wasn't in pieces inside my chest, shattered by the weight of my sorrow and guilt. "If I was more of a man, I would've—"

He cut me off before I could finish the thought. "You would've been killed, along with Alessandra."

I turned to look at him, pulling off the sunglasses I wore to hide how fucked up I was inside. "At least I would be with my wife and son."

"And then what the fuck would I do without you, my friend? Huh?"

"You have Tristan."

"I do," he agreed. "And I have no doubt he would protect me with his life. But Tris is missing something inside of him, Enzo. We both know that. He follows my orders without question. But who will be around to talk me out of doing stupid shit when my temper gets out of control? Who'll be here to remind me there are other things that matter sometimes besides the business? To stop me from becoming my father?" He took my face between his hands and forced me to look at him. "I need you, Enzo. YOU. Don't you dare fucking leave me." His fingers tightened on the sides of my head. "*Swear* it to me."

But I couldn't. I couldn't make him a promise I wouldn't be able to keep. The guilt of what I'd done ate at my insides like worms. I was a coward. And a fool. I belonged in the ground with my family.

"I'm your family, too," Luca said quietly, knowing what I was thinking without my having to say it. "I was your family before you ever met Alessandra. And so was Tristan. Could you forgive yourself if you left me and something happened to one of us?"

His face blurred before me. "No," I admitted. And it was true. I'd never be able to rest in peace with the two of them still here.

"Then swear it to me," he said. "Swear you'll stay here with me always."

I blinked away the tears as the sound of mounds of dirt hitting Alessandra's coffin filled my ears. "I swear," I told him.

And I kept that oath. The days went by, gradually turning into months, and then into years. My grief for my wife and son never left me, but it did get easier to think about them over time. Luca saved my life that day. If he hadn't been there, I had no doubt I would've put my gun to my head right then and there and joined my wife in her grave. In return, I watched over his. And there was never anyone in my life who would make me regret my vow to him.

Until now.

CHAPTER 1

Enzo

Fifteen Years Later

Her face...it was her face that shook my fucking soul.

Not the pastel pink hair. Or the nose ring pierced through her left nostril. Or the slutty outfit that drew my eyes to every inch of creamy flesh it revealed. Or the scent of coconuts and some kind of tropical flower that drifted to my nose.

No. It was her fucking face.

The first thing I noticed was that it was perfectly symmetrical. A slightly wider forehead tapering down to high cheekbones and a firm jawline that rounded gracefully into her strong chin. Her nose wasn't too small, or large, or thin, or long, but the type of nose I often saw in Tristan's drawings of the "perfect" face. At least those he allowed me to see.

But all of that was taken in almost subconsciously as eyes the color of a bright morning fog locked onto mine. Not blue, but not gray, either, with a black ring surrounding the irises. They were outlined with smudgy black liner, making them stand out like a lighthouse in a storm. Dark eyebrows framed them perfectly.

Those eyes saw through the sunglasses I wore as a barrier between me and everyone else I met, and I swayed on my feet as the force of her gaze swept through me like the gust of a hurricane. Only my grip on the hotel door kept me steady.

She smiled with blush painted lips that begged to have my cock between them, and I noticed there was a slight gap between her top two front teeth. Although they weren't discolored, it took me by surprise that in this day and age, there was anyone walking around who hadn't had their teeth forced into submission by braces or some other type of expensive dental work. But I didn't mind it. It gave some character to her otherwise too-perfect features.

"Are you gonna let me in? Or are you gonna leave me standing out here in the hall all damn night?" A flirty demand from those sweet lips.

Her voice was soft, a bit husky, with a slight tremor that was only noticeable to someone who was really paying attention—and I couldn't help but give her my full regard —a direct contrast to the bold words coming out of her mouth.

I raked my eyes over the rest of her to get a better look at what she was wearing. She was petite, coming about to my chin in heels, but not without curves. Full, luscious curves of which I could see plenty. Teardrop-shaped breasts that would spill from my hands, and deliciously rounded hips. The strip of her stomach revealed by the dress was soft and slightly curved. Her legs were full and shapely, tapering down to small ankles and feet in four-inch heels. She would never be a model. No. This one was made for fucking.

My fingers twitched with the urge to touch her, to see if her pale skin felt as smooth and satiny as it looked.

Also, I wasn't completely convinced that the hot pink dress she wore wasn't, in reality, anything more than a roll of bandages she'd wrapped around herself half-haphazardly until it hid only enough to keep her from being arrested for public indecency. The material covered only her nipples and cunt, and barely at that. The only thing keeping her from getting raped in the street was the thigh-length black coat that, when pulled closed, could possibly preserve a portion of her modesty.

I was dying to see the back of that dress.

Tearing my eyes from her body, I realized she was still staring at me expectantly. "Who are you?" I asked her. "Where's Jade?" I was being rude, but this woman was way too fucking distracting. She'd get me killed just watching her walk to my car.

"Jade couldn't make it. She sent me in her place. Is that alright?" She smiled again, but it was a nervous smile that didn't reach her eyes. Something I only noticed now. I searched her face again, and this time I could see the lines of tension around her mouth and eyes. So why was she here?

But I didn't have to ask the question. I knew. It was money. Enough that it kept her from running screaming back down the hall as soon as I'd opened the door.

Was she so desperate she would do something like this? That would explain the dress and the lack of dental work. She didn't look very old. If she was out of high school, I'd be surprised. Without a word, I started to close the door. This little girl, whoever she was, wasn't what I needed tonight.

"Wait!" She threw herself forward and blocked the door with her body. "What-what are you doing? Jade said you needed a date tonight."

"And she was correct. I need a date. Someone I can take to a very important party. Not a cheap fuck from an underage whore."

Something I couldn't quite read flashed across her face before she quickly schooled her expression. "I'm not cheap," she told me, lifting her chin. "My price is the same as Jade's. And I'm not underage. I turned twenty-five two months ago. I just look young." Then she dropped those gorgeous eyes, hiding her expression and lowering her voice as she said, "And I apologize if I had the wrong idea. Jade is sick. And all she told me was that one of her regular clients needed a girl. She neglected to fill me in on the rest of it. I just assumed..." she trailed off.

It didn't escape my notice that she didn't dispute the "whore" part, which surprised me. Even prostitutes on the street begging to suck your dick for a few dollars to support their crack habit would argue the terminology. I tilted my head and stared down at her. The nervous tremor had faded from her voice, and her expression had settled into what I now interpreted as a look of relief. Also, her words were much more articulate than the first impression she'd given me. Which meant she'd been faking the whore act when she'd first arrived. For some reason, a sense of relief flowed through me. But then I frowned. "Am I that monstrous to you?"

Her eyes flew to my face. "I'm sorry?"

Leaning against the wall so I blocked her view of the room, one of the most expensive in the city, I crossed my arms and ankles. "You seem very relieved that you won't have to fuck me tonight."

She stared up at me and blinked a few times. "Could you take off your sunglasses?"

"No."

Her dark eyebrows lifted in surprise at my short answer. "Um. Okay, then." Gathering herself, she wet her lips with the tip of her tongue, drawing my attention to her plump lower lip. I had the sudden urge to bite it until I tasted her blood. My cock, already partially hard, swelled at the thought. Despite what I'd said earlier, I *wanted* to taste her. *All* of her.

She cleared her throat, snapping me out of my fantasy. "It's not that I'm relieved. I mean, I am. But only because this isn't my normal occupation, and I guess I'm a little more nervous than I thought I would be."

I managed to contain my snort of disbelief. "You show up at a strange man's door, dressed the way you are, expecting him to fuck you for money, and you're trying to tell me this isn't why you're here?"

She shook her head. "No. That *is* why I'm here. Just that I've never done...*this* before." She waved her hand in front of her, taking in her outfit, me, and the room behind me.

I'd expected her to be offended by my bluntness. But, instead, her words rang with honesty and a touch of innocence that intrigued me.

"Look," she told me. "You need a date. And I really need a night out. How about you let me run back to Jade's and change and we can start this night over?"

"I don't have time for you to do that. There's somewhere I need to be."

I watched her face as she finally accepted the fact that she wasn't getting my money tonight. After a pause, she stepped back into the hall so she was no longer blocking the door. Pulling her coat closed, she buttoned it up, hiding that delectable body from me. For reasons I couldn't identify, it made me irrationally angry.

"Okay. Well, I apologize for all of this. Really. I do. And please don't blame Jade. It wasn't her fault. I should've asked her to be more specific about what was expected of me. I just assumed—"

"You just assumed your friend is a cheap prostitute who meets men in shady hotels and lets them come wherever they want to for a few hundred bucks?" I couldn't stop the asshole from coming out of my mouth. But something about this woman showing up at a random man's door, a man she knew nothing about, pissed me off. And I was taking it out on her.

She scoffed. "This isn't a shady hotel."

No, it wasn't. It was a very expensive hotel, and I was in the penthouse on the top floor. But that wasn't the point. "I'll be happy to inform Jade exactly what her so-called friends think of her when I see her next." Jade wasn't cheap. She was an escort of the highest class, able to act the part of a lady and fit into any situation I needed her to. Sometimes I fucked her. Most times I didn't. But I always enjoyed her company. This one must be new. She had a lot to learn. And I was being a dick. But I couldn't seem to stop myself.

She gave her head a hard shake, pink hair sliding over her shoulders. "No. That's not...I just...I just didn't know. As I said, this isn't what I normally do. And I'm not from the area, but I needed this...I *really* needed this. The money, I mean," she rushed to say. Her cheeks became flushed as she rambled on. "And Jade needed someone to take her place, and so I volunteered, and it was just all very fast." She looked up at me, her eyes searching for mine behind the dark lenses of my glasses. I'd grabbed them out of habit when I first heard her knock, expecting to walk right out the door with Jade and head out to the party. And now I refused to take them off so she couldn't see the hunger that had started to burn inside of me the moment I'd opened the door and seen *her* standing on the other side. This woman who evoked things inside of me I'd rather not feel.

She lowered her chin. Without another word, she turned to go.

I pulled off my sunglasses and watched her walk away, my eyes falling to her bare legs. There was a discoloration on the inside of one calf. A bruise. Or maybe a burn? Something clenched inside my chest, squeezing tighter the farther away she got. Sliding my glasses back onto my face, I called after her. "Wait."

CHAPTER 2

Enzo

She stopped and turned around, but didn't come back. Her face was carefully blank.

"What's your name?"

"Sera. With an 'e'."

A pretty Italian name for a beautiful woman. "Sera what?"

"Just Sera."

I shoved my hands into the front pockets of my dress slacks in an attempt to disguise the raging hard on she gave me just by standing there in that goddamn non-dress I knew was hiding underneath her coat. "Come back. I need a date, and you're already here." Because I sure as hell wasn't allowing her to run off to someone else who wouldn't think twice about abusing that luscious young body.

She glanced down at herself. "What about the way I'm dressed?"

"I'll buy you a new dress."

"I can't ask you to do that."

"You're not asking me. Consider it part of your payment for the pleasure of your company tonight."

She hesitated, but only for a moment, and I couldn't quite figure out if it was over the offer of a new dress or the fact that she would need to carry through with this night after all that made her pause. Lifting her chin in a gesture I was beginning to recognize as something she did when she was feeling unsure of herself, she walked back over to me with forced confident strides and waited for further instructions.

Good girl.

"Just let me get my coat," I told her. Opening the door all the way and propping it against the wall so I could keep an eye on her, I went inside and got my coat, keys, and cell phone as I tried to talk myself out of taking her with me. This was a bad fucking idea. Sera was much more distracting to me than Jade ever was. It was one of the reasons I used her when I had to go to parties or dinners.

I couldn't afford to have my attention on anything else other than what I was there for, which was usually protecting Luca or gathering information we had no business knowing.

But something had twisted in my gut as I'd watched her walk away with that forlorn expression. I couldn't let her leave like that. At least not tonight. And perhaps, before the evening was through, I'd take her up on her original offer.

My cock pulsed in agreement beneath the cover of my jacket. "Let's go." Taking her hand in mine, I let the door close behind me and led her to the elevator. She needed clothes, and we were already late.

An hour later, with the help of the hotel concierge, Sera was in a new dress fit for the occasion and we'd arrived at the venue.

"This is where the party is?"

The tone of her voice drew my attention. I glanced over at her as we pulled up to the restaurant. "Yes. Why?"

"It looks like an old church."

"It's actually a restaurant, run by an Italian family who came here to America from Italy almost forty years ago. The original owners have passed away, and the kids run it now. Everything inside was brought on the ship from Italy, including the recipes. The Bistecca Alla Fiorentina is some of the best I've ever tasted." I didn't mention that the owners were also very aware of who we were and what we did. We protected them and gave them plenty of business. And in return, they took good care of us when we frequented their restaurant. "We're going to a wedding reception being held here. A distant cousin of mine." It was actually the youngest son of one of our best soldiers. He was way too fucking young to be getting married, but according to his father there'd been no talking him out of it. And the girl he'd just married was Irish, her father a member of the mob in New Orleans, so it made for good neighborly relations.

She smiled, showing off that fascinating gap in her teeth. "It sounds wonderful."

I parked the SUV near the door and ran my eyes over her one last time as she took off her seatbelt. The concierge had taken one look at her and called a boutique near the hotel, who had immediately sent over one of their sales associates with three different dresses to choose from that had all fit Sera almost perfectly. The dress she chose was modest, with short sleeves and a high neckline. Creamy lace with fawn-colored accents, it came to her knees, and with her pastel pink hair and light makeup, it gave her a soft, feminine appearance. Innocent. The only things she still wore that were her own were the nose ring and the shoes. They were nude and matched the new dress better than the scraps she'd been wearing before. "Let me see your coat," I told her. "You won't need it inside. The place is small, and it always gets warm when it fills up with people."

She shrugged out of it, handing it to me without argument. I folded it carefully and laid it on the backseat. As I went to open my door, I caught her eyeing me with a curious expression. "What?"

"Do you ever take off your sunglasses? I mean," she hurried on, "do you need them to see or something? Or do you have sensitive eyes?"

"No," I told her in answer to both questions, then I opened my door and got out, walking around the vehicle to open hers for her. But by the time I arrived, she was already out of the car and waiting for me.

"No for which one?" she asked. "Which question?"

"All of them." Taking her hand, I helped her navigate the rocks in the drive. I told myself it was because I didn't need her to break an ankle. I had no time to take her to the hospital. I wouldn't admit that wasn't the only reason I assisted her.

Her hand felt fragile in mine. The skin soft. Like if I squeezed just a little harder, I'd feel the bones snap beneath my fingers. Absently, I rubbed my thumb along the back, memorizing the texture of her skin.

She stopped when we reached the door, tugging me to a halt. "So who all is going to be at this party? Anything I should know before we go in there? Like, your name, maybe?"

Anger rose within me, swift and unreasonable. "Jade didn't even tell you my name? You allowed a complete stranger to put you in his car and ride off into the middle of fucking nowhere with you?" I took a step closer, crowding her against the doorframe. "What the fuck is wrong with you?"

That came out harsher than I'd intended. I expected her to back up. Maybe start crying. But instead, she raised one eyebrow. "Are you planning to murder me?" she asked with a bland expression.

"Not tonight," I told her when I could speak, and watched with a glimmer of satisfaction as a bit of the color drained from her face. "But you didn't know that."

She shrugged one shoulder. "When do we ever know what will happen to us? I could die at any time. Get hit by a bus. Have an allergic reaction." She eyed me. "Get murdered by someone I thought I could trust."

I stared at her for a moment. She had a point, dammit. "Enzo. My name is Enzo."

She nodded. "Enzo. Okay. Anything else I need to know?"

Her brave front didn't fool me. She was nervous. I could see her pulse fluttering in her throat. "You're a friend of Jade's who was kind enough to fill in for her tonight as my date. That's all anyone needs to know. No one will ask questions. Smile. Be nice. No matter what anyone says to you. Don't cause any trouble."

"Okay. I can do that."

"And don't wander too far from my side." I didn't know why I said this. No one would fuck with her. Not after they saw her walk in with me.

"Alright. Stay by you. Got it." She glanced toward the door when a surge of male laughter rose inside, then swallowed hard and rubbed the chill from her bare arms.

"Hey." Taking her chin in my hand, I turned her face up to mine until I could see her eyes. "Nothing will happen to you tonight. No one will touch you. You have my word." Except me. Sometime between buying her the dress and arriving here, I'd decided that I *would* be taking full advantage of her services tonight. All of them.

"Okay."

Even though she agreed, I didn't let go of her face. Instead, my eyes dropped down to her full lower lip. Before I could think about it, I lowered my head and took it between my teeth, biting down until I heard her whimper and tasted the salty copper of her blood. I ran my tongue over the small wound, then sucked her lip into my mouth before letting go and dropping a light kiss on her mouth.

Sera stared up at me with wide eyes. "What the hell was that?" She hadn't moved. Didn't try to push me away. But when I stepped away, I noticed her arms were partially bent and her hands were fisted.

I couldn't answer her question. Because I didn't know. As I stared down at her and tried to get my lust for this woman under control, I realized a light misty rain had begun to fall. I put my hand to her back and ushered her toward the door. "Come on. We need to go in."

She blinked as though coming out of a trance. "Uh. Yeah. Okay."

I opened the door for her. Lowering her head to watch where she was walking, I didn't miss the way she touched her mouth with the fingertips of her right hand.

"Enzo!"

Dragging my eyes away from the beguiling creature beside me, I stopped in the entryway and greeted our hostess as Sera looked around at the photos of guests and the ceramic knickknacks the family had brought overseas with them. "Marg. How are you? Is everyone behaving?"

"Oh, yes," she said in her soft Italian accent. "They're all being perfect gentlemen. And the ladies look gorgeous. But none are as pretty as this one." She smiled at Sera. "Everyone is in the back room." If she was surprised to see me with someone other than Jade, she gave no sign of it. A professional through and through.

I started to walk forward, following Marg out of the small entryway and into the restaurant, when I realized Sera wasn't with me. Glancing back over my shoulder, I noticed she had moved into the shadows in the corner next to the old-fashioned desk that held framed newspaper clippings and the stand with the sign-in book, her bright eyes wide as she stared at the people inside. "What's wrong?"

Not taking her eyes from the group who had wandered closest to us, she said, "Um. I'm so sorry, Enzo, but I think I need to go home. I'm not feeling well." She turned her attention to me as she started backing away toward the door. "Maybe I'm coming down with whatever it is Jade has." I watched her eyes dart around the room once more, then she gave me a small, apologetic smile and put her head down as she turned to leave.

"Sera. Wait."

"I'm so sorry," she told me. Without waiting for me, she hurried back out the door and into the cold rain that had begun to fall.

I followed her outside. She didn't go toward the SUV. Instead, she was picking her way over the rocks heading to the main road, her arms wrapped around herself in a vain effort to stay warm. "Where the hell do you think you're going?"

"I don't want to ruin your night," she called over her shoulder. "I think I saw a bus stop down here. I'll catch the next one and make my way home."

I had no idea where Jade lived, but I knew it wasn't out here by the lakes. I followed behind her. Did she even have any money to pay for a bus? "Come inside. I'll find you a quiet corner and get you some water or soup or something. Then I'll drive you home as soon as I congratulate the new couple." And talk to a few people to gauge their feelings about Luca taking over as boss.

"No, really. It's okay."

She picked up speed. *Now* she was running from me. I stopped where I was. I wasn't going to chase her down the road like some weak ass, pimply-faced teenager. "For fuck's sake, Sera. STOP!"

She stumbled to a halt, her arms flailing as her ankle twisted beneath her.

I took a quick step forward, but before I could reach her, she straightened, testing her ankle before turning to face me. My arms dropped to my sides. What the fuck was going on with her?

She opened her mouth to speak, but upon seeing the expression on my face, closed it again.

Fuck it. I was getting soaked. And so was she. "I'll take you home. And I'm finished arguing with you, so I wouldn't push it." I held out my hand.

She hesitated, then carefully made her way over to me and took my offer of help. "Thank you," she said quietly, keeping her head down, her wet hair hiding her eyes from me.

My blood ran fast as she submitted to me, and I barely held in my groan. I put her in the car and ran my fingers through my wet hair as I walked around to the driver's side.

I would take her home as I promised.

But not just yet.

CHAPTER 3

Serafina

As soon as I was in the car, I reached around to the back seat and dragged my coat over my lap. Heart racing like I'd just sprinted the Olympic hundred-meter dash, I dropped the porcelain crucifix I'd swiped off the old-fashioned desk into one of the pockets just as Enzo joined me. He glanced over, saw the coat on my lap and the way I was shivering, and cranked the ignition and turned the heat on.

I was glad it was chilly enough to have the coat. And I would return the cross the first chance I could. Taking it had been an automatic reaction to the rise of panic I'd experienced when I saw the others who were attending the wedding dinner. Something I'd had no control over. A self-defense mechanism, if you will, that comes on whenever I get too nervous in a situation. Or too emotional in any form, really. At least that's what my therapists told me. I'd been doing it ever since I was a kid, and after years of doctor's visits and behavioral therapy, I still had no idea why or how to stop myself from stealing.

Enzo turned the heat up more as the engine warmed up. But I wasn't shivering because of the cold. Although the temperature had dropped a bit with the rain, it was still pretty mild for Austin this time of year. No, I was shaking was for an entirely different reason.

I was in shock.

I think.

I'd literally just escaped the lion's mouth.

Why, _why_, didn't I ask Jade more about this guy before I offered to take her place tonight as his date? All she'd told me was that he was a big spender, he'd never hit her in anger, didn't ask a lot of questions, always made sure she made it home safe, and that he took care of her in bed. But I should've asked more questions. Or hell, maybe she didn't know who he really was. Was that possible? No. It couldn't be. If he took her to functions like this, there was no fucking way she couldn't know he was in the mob.

I'd never been so grateful I didn't tell him my full name.

My thoughts were interrupted when Enzo took off his sunglasses, grabbed a soft cloth from the console, and started to dry them. I stared at his profile, suddenly wishing he would look at me so I could see his eyes. I wondered what color they were. Brown, if I had to guess by his coloring. Maybe hazel.

No. It was better if he didn't look directly at me. Judging by the firm set of his jaw, he wasn't very happy with me. Not that he'd done so much as crack a smile all night, so it was kind of hard to tell. But in any case, I didn't need him to look too closely at me right now. And not just because I'd stolen a knickknack. But because I was never very good at hiding my emotions. And right now, I was scared shitless. He'd see it on my face, and he would start asking questions. Questions I wasn't ready to answer.

I looked away quickly and stared straight out of the front windshield at the front of the restaurant as he put his glasses back on and shifted into reverse. It had smelled wonderful inside, and my stomach growled in protest. I'd like to come back here sometime and eat when it wasn't being overrun by mafia men who knew my father.

My eyes widened as the front door swung open and a man I'd met only once before stepped outside. He threw his arms up in the air in the universal sign for "where are you going?" and then scowled up at the sky as the rain went from a drizzle to a downpour. I ducked my head and hid my face before his attention came back to us. My throat thickened until I couldn't even swallow and my heart tried to gallop right out of my chest as I waited for Enzo to notice him.

Oh, my god. I was completely and utterly fucked. And not in the way I was hoping for when I'd set out tonight.

But, by some grace of that same god, Enzo either ignored the man or didn't see him and continued to back away, cutting the wheel so my side of the car was closest to the restaurant before pulling forward and making his way down the drive to the main road. I silently said a Hail Mary that the windows were tinted as dark as they were.

"You're quiet."

I'd been staring out the window ever since we'd left the restaurant, lost in my thoughts as I listened to the sound of the rain hitting the windows and the squeak of the windshield wipers swinging back and forth, and it startled me when he spoke. I'd almost forgotten he was there, and that caught me by surprise considering how close I was to being caught just from sitting next to this man. Plus, I wasn't one to daydream. I was always aware of my surroundings and who was in my near vicinity. I'd had to be. "Um, yeah. I'm sorry." I didn't know why I was apologizing. I was allowed to not be forced into idle conversation if I didn't want to speak, and he was only making an observation.

I felt more than saw his eyes run over the entire length of my body, and suddenly it was entirely too hot underneath my coat, and the space between our seats was way too close. I couldn't seem to take a full breath.

"How are you feeling?"

It was on the tip of my tongue to say "strangely flustered" before I remembered I was supposed to be ill. "Better now that I'm away from all the food smells. And since there's no way in hell I could be pregnant, I think it's likely I'm coming down with Jade's stomach bug." The lie burned the back of my throat. In reality, Jade wasn't sick at all. She was out on a date with another client. And I wasn't sick, either. But he didn't need to know that.

Enzo kept his eyes straight ahead as he navigated the winding road in the rain. "I'd like to take you back to the hotel. And I'd like you to spend the night with me."

Such simple words, spoken in a straightforward manner and without any hint of emotion. Yet my pulse sped up and my stomach tightened like I'd just gone over the peak of a roller coaster track, and I was now speeding back down the other side and doing loop-ty loops. I looked down at my lap before glancing over at him. He still wasn't looking at me, but watching the slick road in front of him. This was what I'd expected when I'd begged Jade to let me take her place. But now that the moment was here, I found I wasn't as prepared as I thought I'd been. I cleared my throat. *Get it together, Sera.* "Aren't you worried I'll vomit all over your hotel room? Or get you sick?"

"No. I don't get sick."

When I was silent for too long, he said, "I'll double your rate."

My eyes widened as I stared at him. That was a hell of a lot of money. But I couldn't. Not with him. I needed to end this date and stay far, far off his radar. "No. No, that's not why I—"

"I want you in my bed tonight, Sera." Slowing down, he stopped at a light and turned his head to look at me. Even though I couldn't see his eyes, I could feel the way they burned and see the tension in his jaw. Unintentionally— or maybe not—my eyes dropped to his lap, and I quickly averted them when I saw the thick proof of what he was saying. "I'll get you whatever you need for your stomach, but I want you to stay with me."

It sounded more like an order than a request, and I felt my hackles go up in response. However, I strove to keep my tone as unemotional as his when I told him in a firm tone, "I'm sorry, Enzo. But I'm really not feeling well. I just need to go home."

The car behind us laid on his horn, and Enzo glanced into the rearview mirror, then stepped on the gas and returned his attention to the road.

I took a deep breath and turned my head to stare out the window. He seemed to accept my answer this time because he said nothing else. However, he also didn't ask for directions to where I was staying, and I knew he didn't know where that was since he'd just met me tonight, so he must be taking me back to his hotel. That was fine. Once we arrived, I could catch an Uber. I don't think Jade wanted her clients to know where she lived, anyway, and I was staying with her until I could save up enough money to start over somewhere else.

Despite the fact that I was playing with fire, I had to admit I was both relieved and disappointed that he'd given in so easily. An awkward silence stretched between us, at least on my end, and I searched for something to say. "How can you see to drive in those things?" I was genuinely curious.

"I can see fine. I'm used to them."

"I guess I'll have to take your word for it." He didn't respond, but I continued to try to distract him from his mission of getting me in his bed. "Do you wear them to hide something? Do you have a nasty birthmark or scar or something?" Jade hadn't said anything about him being disfigured. But that didn't mean he wasn't. To her, these guys she spent her time with were nothing but dollar signs. "It wouldn't matter to me at all. I'm just curious."

"Or something," was all he said.

Pulling up in front of the hotel, he turned off the SUV and came around the front to open my door, giving me his hand to help me out. "Thank you," I murmured. "I'll just call an Uber from the lobby and be out of your hair." He gave his keys to the valet, and I put on my coat as we walked up to the doors. "Again, I'm sorry I ruined your night."

"It's alright," he replied. "I actually hate weddings."

I smiled. "Most guys do." Then I held out my hand. "It was nice meeting you," I lied. "I'll pay you back for the dress." How I was going to do this, I had no idea. But since I hadn't earned it, it was really the right thing to do.

"That's not necessary. Consider it a gift. And my offer to stay still stands."

"Perhaps another time," I told him in a firm voice.

He stared down at me for so long I began to feel awkward standing there, holding my hand out. I was about to pull it back when he reached out and wrapped his long fingers around mine. Turning it until my palm faced up, he brought my hand up to his mouth and pressed a soft kiss to the inside of my wrist, his lips lingering over my pulse point as though he could feel how fast it fluttered.

My lips parted on a soft gasp as my nipples hardened and the muscles deep in my womb tightened sharply. I barely stopped myself from rubbing my thighs together to ease the sudden ache between them.

Pulling my hand from his, I gave him a small, apologetic smile for my impending rudeness and without another word, I turned and walked into the lobby to call my ride.

While I waited at the front desk to ask the girl behind the counter to make the call for me, I didn't turn around to see where Enzo was, not even when I heard the sound of his dress shoes on the marble floors. His steps never faltered as he headed to the elevator on the other side of the lobby. But then again, why should they? I was just some strange woman with pink hair he'd had the misfortune of getting blue balls from tonight. I was very lucky he was such a gentleman about it all. And there was no reason he shouldn't forget about me just as soon as I was out of his sight.

So why did I feel such a deep stab of rejection?

As I waited for my Uber, I silently scolded myself. I was being foolish. This guy wasn't someone I'd met on a night off at the club and had some kind of immediate connection with. He was a client. And a disappointed one at that. There was no reason in hell he'd spare me one more thought. And no reason why I should want him to.

The phone rang, and the little blonde girl who was working the desk walked over and answered. I didn't pay much attention to what she was saying until she hung up and I realized she was trying to get my attention. "Yes?" I asked her.

"That was Mr. Delligatti. He would like you to know that your ride is on its way and the cost of your Uber has been taken care of. Also, that he will see you here Tuesday night at eight o'clock sharp."

Enzo *Delligatti*. I knew that name. From...somewhere...

My breath caught in my lungs. I couldn't believe I'd been so stupid as to not have recognized him the moment he opened the door to his room. A large, hard-looking man with spiky dark hair and sunglasses who obviously had money to burn. And his name. How many Enzos were there in the city of Austin that fit that description?

Even though I'd never actually met him, he was infamous in our world. The right-hand man of Luca Morelli, the underboss of the Italian mafia in this area. It was said Luca was growing more powerful than his father, and was putting himself in a position to take over as boss. Fuck.

Fuck!

I gripped the crucifix in my pocket tightly. *It's okay. He doesn't know who you are. Just keep it together.* "After I leave, please give him my apologies. I'm not available Tuesday night."

Luckily, my Uber chose that moment to pull up to the curb. "But please thank him for the ride home." Leaving her staring after me with her mouth hanging open in shock, I rushed out of the hotel and got into the car.

Yeah, even the hotel staff knew no one ever said no to Enzo Delligatti.

At least, not until tonight.

CHAPTER 4

Serafina

I was waiting for Jade at the kitchen table when she got home. From there, I had a perfect view of the door. It was a small apartment. My room was about twelve steps away, and it contained a couch, a television, and a corner where I'd piled all of my stuff. Otherwise known as the "living room." My heels were kicked off and I was working on my third glass of red wine when I heard her key in the lock.

"Why the fuck didn't you tell me who he was?" I was on her as soon as she walked in the door.

One perfectly sculpted dark eyebrow rose as her bright green eyes took in my new dress and tipsy state. With her black hair, pale skin, and model-esque figure wrapped in a bright red sheath dress under a perfectly fitted black coat, Jade was stunningly gorgeous in her stiletto heels.

No wonder Enzo had looked disappointed when he'd opened the door to find *me* standing there. I wasn't bad looking, but I didn't look like *that*. I had what my grandmother used to tell me were "good childbearing hips."

"What are you talking about? I told you who he was."

"But you didn't tell me *who* he was," I insisted. "You didn't tell me where he was taking me. And that someone there might recognize me. Hell, you didn't even tell me his name!"

"You didn't ask." Jade set her purse on the small table by the door that was used as a catch-all for bags, keys, mail, and anything else we didn't have a place for. Then she shrugged out of her coat and hung it on the hook beside it, taking an envelope out of the pocket. "He said he needed a date for a party. That's all I knew. He doesn't give me details."

"You didn't even bother to tell me that much," I accused. "Do you know what I wore to his hotel?"

She spun toward me, an expression of horror on her face. "Don't tell me you wore the pink dress."

"I wore the pink dress."

Her hands flew up to cover her ears, and she whacked herself in the head with the envelope. "I told you not to tell me!"

Grabbing the bottle of wine, I refilled my glass.

"I told you he had money, Sera. *Money.* You don't wear the pink dress to a date with a guy who has money."

"Well, Jade, how the fuck am I supposed to know that? I'd never done this before. He had to go buy me a *new* dress so I would look presentable enough to be on his arm." I frowned at her. "And what does having money matter? They all have money, or they wouldn't be able to afford us!"

"But there's money, and then there's *money*. The first ones are your typical guys who have a hard time getting dates and wanna get laid. They're either too nerdy, too ugly, too shy, or whatever. They only pay for the hour or two they need to wine, dine, and fuck you, and they don't tip. The ones in the second group are really just lonely guys who want some company because they're afraid that every woman they meet only cares about how rich they are, and not them as a person. Money is no object to them. I once had a guy like my company so much he paid me triple my rate to keep me at his house for a week just so he could pretend I was his while I watched television and made dinner for him."

"We *do* only care about how rich they are."

"Yes, but with us, they know that going in. They'd rather pay for an escort than take a chance on catching feelings for someone who's only after what's in their bank accounts. With us, it's all out there in the open. They know what to expect. No complications. We smile, we laugh at their jokes, we don't argue with them, we look at them like they're the only man in the room, and the ones that want to fuck us can do so without worrying we're gonna show up on their doorstep the next day with a casserole dish hoping they're 'the one.' Mr. Delligatti is in that category."

I set down my wine glass a little too hard. "I've never made a casserole for any man."

Jade opened the cabinet to the right of the small stove and grabbed a glass for herself, then joined me at the table, slapped the envelope down in front of me, and poured the rest of the bottle into hers. "It's an expression."

"Did you ever show up at some guy's door with a homemade dinner and hearts in your eyes?" I couldn't see the Jade I knew now doing something like that, but when do you really ever know people?

"Hell no," she told me. "They stalked me. Not the other way around."

"That I can believe." I sighed heavily and ran my finger around the rim of my glass as I looked up at my new friend from beneath my lashes. I glanced at the envelope. "What's this?"

"Mr. Delligatti wired over the money for your time tonight."

Curious, I opened the envelope and my jaw dropped open as I thumbed through the stack of hundreds inside.

"Holy fuck." Closing the envelope, I shoved it back at her. "You need to return it to him."

"What? Why?"

"Because I didn't fulfill my obligation. We never even made it to the party."

She gave me a naughty smile. "I figured that out as soon as you told me you'd worn the pink dress."

I shook my head. "We didn't do that either. I bailed on him. Cut the date short."

"Why the hell would you do that? What about your...little problem?" She paused and set down her glass to give me a sympathetic look. "Was he not interested? Was it the pink hair?"

Taking a drink for courage, I filled her in on what had happened. "I showed up there expecting maybe we'd have a drink or two, a little small talk—"

"Oh, Mr. Delligatti doesn't do small talk."

Sarcasm dripped from my voice when I said, "Yeah. I figured that out real fast."

The corners of her red lips tipped up as she fought her smile, until finally she took a sip of wine to hide it. "Sorry," she said when she put her glass back down. "Go on."

"As I was saying, I thought, you know, we'd kick it around a bit and then get down to the business at hand—ridding me of my involuntary, imposed virginity. So, imagine my surprise when I found out he didn't want to fuck me. I mean, he did. But first, he wanted to take me to a party. And not just any party. A wedding reception. To welcome a *made man's* new bride to the *family*." I didn't have to tell her what family I was talking about. I'd told Jade the second week I knew her that I was the daughter of a wannabe mafia boss and that I'd moved down here from Dallas to get the fuck away from him.

I didn't tell her that he'd kept me a near prisoner my entire life because he was so afraid someone would steal my "innocence" before he could auction it off to the highest bidder. I also didn't tell her that I'd run away from home, so to speak. I was a grown woman, and legally could live wherever the hell I wanted, but that didn't mean much in my family. If my father found out where I was, all he had to do was send a few of his thugs down here to Austin to get me, and before I knew it, I'd be locked in my room again. It was nothing short of a miracle that I'd made it to this age without him finding some disgusting old gangster to give me to. He needed something before he could do that, though, to make the best possible match. A better position in the family. Apparently, these days, virgins alone weren't enough to elevate you.

He'd finally attained that position just recently by killing off a few select colleagues without anyone knowing it was him, which elevated him to the position of underboss in a relatively short time. I just thanked god that I was an only child and that my mother was dead, so she didn't have to see the things I would resort to doing just to get away from him. Not that there was anything wrong with what Jade did. Hell, to each their own. I certainly was in no position to judge anyone. And although I wasn't looking to become an escort, filling in for her just this one night was supposed to help me get rid of the one thing my father valued me for...

My hymen.

"I'm sorry things didn't work out for you tonight," she told me. "I'm booked again tomorrow night. And this guy is not mafia. I can guarantee it. He's the owner of the newest tech company. The one that has that new high-rise downtown. You know the one I mean?"

I did know. And I'd read an article about that guy. All about how he was now one of the youngest billionaires in Austin. The article had also had a picture.

"Thanks, but no thanks," I told her. There was no way in hell I was going to finally lose my virginity to a guy who looked like he was fourteen. "Enzo asked me...no, that's not right...he *ordered* me—through the concierge—to come back and meet him in the lobby of his hotel on Tuesday night at eight."

Jade grinned. "Well, there you go! You'll have a second chance."

I looked at her like she'd lost her mind. "I'm not going to go."

"Why not?"

"Because he's mafia, Jade!"

She raised her eyebrows as if to say, "And?"

I rubbed my forehead with my fingertips. "You just don't get it. I have to stay away from him. If he figures out who I am, my father will be the next to know, and his men will be down here to collect me in a hot minute."

"I think you're just being paranoid. If he didn't recognize you right off, how will he know who you are unless you tell him?"

"No, Jade. I'm not." I laid my palms flat down on the table and tried to emphasize just how wrong she was. "You don't understand because you only play in that world. You don't live in it. The mafia is like a giant spiderweb across this entire country. The entire globe! Every big city has its boss, the one that calls the shots, but they all work together whenever they need to. The Italians, the Russians, the Irish... And it's a big sausage fest. For as family oriented as they are, very few women have any power within this network. We're treated like possessions. Wives are there to cook the meals and raise the kids and smile pretty so the men can pat themselves on the back on what good providers they are. How manly they are out there playing gangster while the little woman waits for them at home, barely staying one step ahead of the FBI and a life in prison. Or worse, getting gunned down in the streets, leaving their families alone with no means to provide for themselves. So they have to depend on the boss to make sure they're taken care of. And they're not allowed to leave the 'family.' Ever."

"I didn't realize," she said quietly. "I mean, I've seen the movies. And I know that organized crime exists, but I've never been involved, other than to be someone's arm candy. I'm shooed away to go powder my nose when the men I'm with have to talk amongst themselves. I only see the glamour of it all, not the reality."

Sighing heavily, I sat back. "I know. I'm sorry. I didn't mean to unload on you."

She gave me a small smile. "So, what are you going to do?"

"I think from now on I'm just gonna stick to my waitressing job at the club. And who knows?" I smiled. "Maybe I'll meet someone, and I can have a normal one-night stand like everyone else. I just won't get paid for it."

Jade finished off her glass of wine and stood up to put it in the sink. "Are you sure?"

"I'm sure."

"Alright," she said as she passed me on the way to the bedroom. "But keep the money. You gave him your time. You earned it. And if you change your mind, just let me know."

"I will," I called after her. "Thanks."

"Night!"

"Goodnight," I called after her.

When I was alone once again, I got up from the table and washed both of our glasses and turned them upside down in the drying rack. Finished, I wiped down the counter, rinsed out the sponge, and then leaned against the sink and stared at the envelope of money lying in the middle of the table.

Slowly, I walked over to it...and then left it where it was as I got my sleeping clothes from the couch and went to the half bath off the kitchen to brush my teeth and get ready for bed.

When Jade had offered to let me stay with her and brought me here so I could get out of the cheap hotel I was in, I couldn't hide my surprise. With the kind of money she made, I'd expected something much bigger and fancier. And I knew what she made because she'd come into the club where I worked alone one night bitching about a date who'd stiffed her.

But the place was in a newer building in a nice part of the city, and Jade, I'd discovered, was a practical girl underneath it all. It was the reason she'd gotten into her line of work. Why slave from nine to five when you could have rich men—or women—take you out to parties, buy you fancy clothes and five star meals, and then pay you just for the honor of your company? The sex was an added bonus for her. And she had enough of a reputation within the industry that she could pick and choose who she slept with, so all in all, not a bad gig.

But even though Jade was always talking up how great the job of being an escort was, it wasn't the life for me. Being around rich people made me nervous. And when I got nervous, I developed a tick of sorts...

Walking over to my coat where it hung on the rack beside Jade's, I stuck my hand down into the right front pocket and pulled out the porcelain crucifix I'd lifted from the restaurant. Jesus hung from the cross with his eyes closed, a crown of thorns on his head and each hair perfectly in place. There was even a little blood painted on his hands and feet to add that realistic feel. I didn't know why I took it. I barely remembered doing it. It had no value to me. No meaning. I didn't need it. And yet, there it was. Judging me.

Tears filled my eyes as I shoved back into my coat pocket. Surely, I was going straight to hell for all the things I'd stolen in my life. I'd look up the restaurant online tomorrow and take it back as soon as they opened. I could pretend I'd lost my phone or something and thought I'd left it there. Or maybe I could just put in the mail anonymously with an apology letter. Surely the family who ran it wouldn't remember everyone who'd been at the party. And as soon as it was back in its rightful place, I'd stop at the catholic church on the corner and go to confession. It would be my first time there, so I wouldn't have to go into a long explanation of how I'd been doing this my entire life and couldn't stop, no matter how much I wanted to.

The response the priests always gave me was to pray. Just pray and everything would be better. It was their fucking answer to everything.

But praying hadn't saved me in this life, no matter how much time I spent on my knees.

Maybe it would help me out in the next one.

CHAPTER 5

Enzo

"**Y**ou alright, Enz?"

No. I wasn't fucking alright. I felt like punching the wall, despite the fact that I'd just spent two hours in Luca's gym taking out my frustration on the punching bag while fighting the insane urge to fist my cock and jack off in the bathroom. *Again.* At the rate I was going, the damn thing would be nothing but raw, bloody skin.

I was too old to be so jacked up over a woman. But I couldn't get the picture of Sera in that fucking scrap of a pink dress out of my head. Or in the creamy lace one that hugged her ass and tits. I shifted on the couch, trying to adjust myself discreetly in my pants, and glad I was sitting down so the raging erection I had wasn't immediately apparent. "I'm fine."

Tristan studied my face and read my mood accurately, as usual. He also knew me well enough to know when it was better to change the subject. "How was the reception?"

My head fell back against the couch cushion. Just the night I was trying not to think about. "I didn't go. But I had the concierge at the hotel send over an apology and an expensive gift."

He gave me a thoughtful look and ambled over to the table against the far wall of Luca's office, where he helped himself to some ice water. There was a bottle of expensive whiskey sitting there, Luca's drink of choice, but Tristan didn't imbibe. Not for as long as I've known him, which was going on thirty-three years now. "I thought you were going to make an appearance?"

"I was. I did. But my date wasn't feeling well, so I took her home. We left as soon as we got there," I explained. "Barely even made it in the door."

Joining me at the new sitting area in front of the desk, thanks to Veda wanting somewhere she could curl up with her schoolbooks while Luca worked, he sat on the opposite end of the couch. "I hope it's nothing serious with Jade."

Jesus fucking Christ. I tried to keep a grip on my patience. He was just asking questions. I should be grateful he was being so talkative, because when he got too quiet, it was time to worry. "It wasn't Jade."

Both eyebrows rose. "Did something happen between you two?"

His shock at my statement wasn't surprising. Jade had been my steady companion for shit like this for going on four years now. She was stunning, mature, educated, not too chatty, and knew when to disappear to the ladies' room without my having to tell her to. I shook my head. "No. She wasn't feeling well and sent a friend in her stead." A little girl with ocean eyes and bubble gum hair who stole a figurine from the entryway of the restaurant when she thought I wasn't watching. An old-looking crucifix that had probably been brought over from Italy with everything else in that place. A little girl who didn't know how to dress, or how to show up when she was ordered to. Instead, she had the fucking balls to very politely tell me no when her presence was requested.

The only problem was she wasn't a little girl at all. Not with a body like that. The curves of her breasts and hips peeking out of that dress still haunted me. I've been walking around with a fucking semi in my pants since the night she showed up at my door.

I forced myself to refocus on the conversation. "But she must've gotten the same thing Jade had." I leaned forward with my elbows on my knees and took off my sunglasses so I could rub my eyes. "Anyway, I didn't go. So there's nothing to report."

Finally, Tristan took the hint. "Do you know what this is all about?" he asked, indicating this meeting Luca had called us into.

I shook my head and pulled out my phone to check the time. "But we'll find out soon enough."

No sooner had the words left my mouth than Luca walked into his office. I noticed right away that he seemed distracted. After greeting us with a nod, he went directly to the whiskey and poured himself a generous glass, then joined us in the seating area in front of his desk, taking a seat in one of the two plush chairs on the other side of the glass coffee table.

"Is Veda okay?" I asked. "Is something going on?"

He shook his head. "She's fine. Getting ready to go to the tutoring lab at the college to get some help with one of her classes."

I stood up to escort her.

"Enzo, sit," Luca told me, gesturing toward the couch cushion I'd just abandoned.

I hesitated. "Did you want Tris to go?"

"No, I need both of you to hear this. I have three of the guards taking her just for today."

"What's going on?" I unbuttoned my jacket and sat back down.

He took a sip of his whiskey and reached over and pulled a file off his desk, laying it on the table between us. He opened it and spun around a few of the photos that were inside so we could see them. They were snapshots of Ciro Cordaro walking into a club, a made man who'd been giving our associates up in Dallas a hard time. "What's he doing now?"

"He's overstepped. Again. And now he's raising hell, saying his daughter has been kidnapped."

"Was she?" Tristan asked.

He shook his head. "I've heard nothing that would lead me to think that's the case. Maybe she just wanted to get away from her father before she got caught in his crossfire. Maybe for her own reasons. In any case, she didn't feel the need to tell him she was leaving."

"So why is this our problem?" I asked him. "She probably ran off with her current fuck or something. Or she's staying with a friend."

"It's not." Luca rifled through the photos and papers in the file until he found what he was looking for. "However, it was asked of us to keep an eye out for her, just in case. And to encourage the ongoing relationship we have with the family in Dallas, I told my father I would handle it." He found the photo he was looking for and pulled it out from between the others. "Here she is. The photo was taken about a year ago when she graduated from college, but from what I understand, she hasn't changed much."

His words echoed in my head, muffled, as if I was hearing them through a glass wall as I stared at the girl in the picture. She had long, dark hair and was wearing a graduation gown with cords around her neck. Her cap was hanging from the fingertips of one hand. Her father was in the photo with her, but he wasn't touching her. He wasn't even smiling. There was no pride in his eyes, just an overall expression of annoyance that he was required to be there.

But all of that was noticed subconsciously. She looked different. Even younger and more innocent. But I knew that face. That perfect, stunning face. There was no makeup. No nose piercing. But it was her. It was Sera.

"Her name is Serafina," Luca said. "People call her Fina."

"Or Sera," I murmured.

Luca glanced up at me. "Possibly. But I was told she goes by Fina."

I picked up the photo, studying the girl in it as Luca continued talking. "I told her father I'd do what I could to see if she was in the area, but honestly, I think it's a waste of fucking time. If she really ran off on him, she could be anywhere by now. She's probably not even in the fucking state."

I realized I was staring at her too long and handed the picture off to Tristan before it looked suspicious. "And if we find her?" he asked. "Is Mr. Cordaro just wanting to know she's safe, or does he want her returned?" He handed the photo back to Luca. No one mentioned the fact that if she'd graduated from college, she was of legal age to make her own choices. Those rules didn't matter in the world of most mafia men. Especially the older generations.

Luca put the photo back inside the folder and closed it. "If we spot her, we're to call her father and he'll send a couple of his soldiers down here to retrieve her. Apparently, he'd just arranged a marriage for her, but was unable to tell her before she disappeared."

My heart sped up and a red haze clouded the corners of my vision as I imagined some fat old man groping her tits and ass. "Maybe she did know, and that's why she ran. Maybe she doesn't want to get married."

"Not our problem," Luca told me shortly.

I don't know why I didn't tell him right away that I knew where she was. Or, at the very least, that I could find her easily. All I knew was that the thought of handing her off to some other man had my hands shaking and my guts twisted in a knot. I concentrated on my breathing, keeping it steady and even as Tristan and Luca talked about all of the trouble Sera's father was causing in Dallas. Like Luca, he was making moves to try to get himself positioned as the next boss. Unlike Luca, he was doing it by taking out the wrong people and causing even more rife within the organization. Also, unlike Luca, Cero was in no way, shape, or form the type of person you wanted running anything. Especially not when your life could be on the line.

I tried to focus on what they were saying until my heartbeat slowed, but it was no use. I had to warn her. "I need to make a call."

Luca stopped talking and looked over at me, his blue eyes more curious than angry at the interruption.

"Sorry," I told him. "I just remembered I needed to check on something at the club for you before the girls get there."

Concern crossed his features. Luca didn't like anything or anyone threatening his workers. "Is there an issue I need to be aware of?"

I shook my head and stood up. "I don't think so. Something showed up on the security camera last night. Probably just some kids fucking with the backdoor of the club, but I want to make sure we have extra security tonight, just in case."

Luca gave me a nod. "Go do what you need to do. Tris can handle doing a search for the daughter on his own."

Goddammit. I didn't have much time. Tristan would hunt her down like a wolf on the trail of a wounded deer, and he wouldn't stop until he found her. I needed to get to her first and find out what the hell was going on before I allowed anyone to turn her back over to her father.

CHAPTER 6

Enzo

My cell was at my ear before I'd even gotten out of the house. I kept my voice low. "Jade, it's Enzo. I need you to tell me where Sera is, and I need you to do it right fucking now."

She wouldn't tell me shit. Not even when I promised her a very large cash gift for handing over the information. I was told if Sera wanted to see me again, she would let me know herself. I had to admire her loyalty, and I would hope that she would show the same to me if the occasion ever arose. But that didn't help me right now.

A tingling ribbon of fear snaked its way through me, and I didn't understand why. It made no sense. I barely knew the girl. Running on autopilot, I climbed into the SUV and took off toward the strip club Luca owned to collect the cash and order more security for the bullshit reason I gave him. He didn't make it a habit to check the security videos. I was the one who did that, so I should be safe there. I ignored the twinge of guilt I felt for lying to my friend and picked up my cell to call my tracker.

After making it clear that he would be the next one to disappear if he breathed a word of this to anyone, anyone at all, I gave him Sera's first and last name, appearance, age, and last known location.

Fifteen minutes later, my phone rang. There was no record of a Serafina Cordaro anywhere in the area. No apartment rental records or credit card charges. That made sense. Working as an escort, she most likely got paid in cash, so there'd be no bank or credit accounts in her name. Not if she was smart.

I smiled to myself, thanked him for his time, and ended the call. The escort business. That was it. There was an upscale club where Jade and other high-end escorts brought their dates. Kind of a *if you know, you know,* kind of place. Nothing official. But it was in Luca's territory. As a matter of fact, Jade had me meet her there the first time I'd hired her. She'd told me she and the other girls, or guys, often met new clients there as it was a public place and very discreet. If Sera was getting into the business, chances were, I would find her there.

Eventually.

Red hot rage flared inside of me, heating my blood until my hands gripped the wheel and my knuckles turned white. The same rage I'd been fighting since the night she ran off. It made no sense. I'd only known the girl a total of a few hours. I'd hardly spoken to her and hadn't so much as kissed her. And yet, in that time, she'd managed to crawl under my skin and nest within the empty cavity of my chest like she fucking belonged there.

Or maybe I was just bored with Jade and all of the other women I met who were either as cold and polished as marble or who thought being the wife of a mafia man would be easy. Nothing but days of shopping and gossiping with the other wives while being draped in furs and jewels. Women who only cared about the money. And Sera was something different. Something fresh and new that hadn't been hardened by the business yet. And this urgency I felt to get to her was because I didn't want her to disappear before I'd had a taste.

It took me over two hours to finish my business with Luca's strip club because of an issue with the liquor shipment. By the time I got out of there, a strange sense of dread was making my skin itch. I'd wanted to arrive early to catch Sera before she went into work. If, in fact, that was where she would be. If not, then my plan was to ask everyone at the club about her until I found someone who wasn't as loyal as Jade. I just needed an address, a phone number, anything. Just some way of getting in contact with her. I needed to know if she was, in fact, the missing mafia princess. Although I didn't see how she couldn't be. And if she was, then what the fuck was she doing whoring herself out to clients like myself who were members of the organization and knew her father. Or at least knew of him. Was this shit she was doing some kind of vendetta against the business that created her father? Or a way to choose a husband for herself? Because if he found out any one of us dared to lay a finger on her, he would demand retribution.

When I arrived, the place was in full swing, despite the fact it was still early in the evening. Done in black and silver with soft lighting and live musicians playing soothing tones on the piano or acoustic guitar, the place was sleek and rich looking without being gaudy, and allowed for both dancing and conversation. Tonight there was a girl on the piano singing a passable version of Uninvited by Alanis Morissette.

Gorgeous women in glittering dresses who didn't already have dates sat at the bar or wandered the room until they caught the eye of one of the gentlemen in tailored suits who had come there to have a few drinks and conversation, and possibly a date for the night. A pretty thing to have on his arm and show off to his friends. Or if he wished, to sink his dick into without worrying if she was going to tell his wife. The girls who worked here were professionals, and normally, I appreciated that.

But not tonight.

After speaking to half of the ladies in the room and getting nowhere, I went to the bar and ordered a double shot of their best whiskey. "I'll be over there," I told the bartender, pointing at a small table in the corner. I was getting frustrated. A few of them were willing enough to talk for a fee, but swore they knew nothing of another girl who worked with them that fit Sera's description.

How a girl with pink hair and that face could go without being noticed was beyond me.

Pulling out my phone, I checked in with Luca and Tristan while I waited for my drink, until the sound of shattering glass to my right made me lift my head with a scowl. The first thing I saw was my whiskey smashed all over the fucking floor, and I cursed under my breath. My eyes met those of the server who couldn't hang onto her tray.

Her blue-gray eyes were wide with shock—and perhaps a hint of fear—as she stared at me, the empty tray in her hands and the floor near her feet covered in shards of glass. Her pink hair was up in pigtails tied with silver and black ribbons, her eyes were lined to look wide and innocent, and there was a lollipop in her mouth. I allowed my eyes to rove over her hungrily, taking in the silver baby doll dress she wore that barely contained her tits or covered her ass. It had a deep neckline and little cap sleeves that fell off her bare shoulders and black ruffles under the skirt that made it poof out. Her legs were covered in black tights that came just over her knees and left her smooth thighs bare, and she had black stilettos on her feet.

She blinked a few times, then crouched down and started picking up the broken glass, turning her side to me so I could see the black ruffled panties she wore underneath the dress.

I jumped up from my table, sending my chair crashing back into the wall, and grabbed her wrist before she could cut herself on the glass. "Stop," I ordered. "Someone else can clean that up."

"I *am* that someone," she gritted out. Sera looked up at me with tears in her eyes. "I'm going to be fired," she said around the ball of candy stuck in her cheek. It pushed her cheek out like the swollen head of my cock would, which I'm sure was the idea.

I tried, and failed, to push the image out of my mind. "No, you're not."

She yanked her arm from my grasp and went back to picking up glass. "I am! This is the second time I've dropped my drinks since I started here. And Tom told me the first time it happened that if it happened again, I would be fired. It wasn't even my fault that first time. Some guy grabbed my ass, and I totally wasn't expecting it. He took me by surprise is all, and my tray went flying..."

She was babbling and swatting my hands away as I tried to stop her from cutting herself, until finally I stood and caught the attention of the bartender so he could send someone over with a broom. Reaching down, I hauled her to her feet beside me. "Drop the fucking glass, Sera. Someone is coming to clean it up." She was making more of a scene by fighting with me. "LEAVE IT," I ordered when she tried to pull away from me to keep cleaning.

Finally, she stopped trying to get me off her and allowed me to pull her over to my table. "Have a seat," I told her.

She pulled the sucker from her mouth. "I can't," she said without looking at me. "I have other tables, and I need those tips before he fires me."

"They can wait. And you won't lose your job. I'll talk to your boss. Everything will be fine."

She glanced up at me, then at the custodian who'd appeared to clean up the mess. "Don't you want another drink?"

Catching the eye of the bartender, I gestured for him to send two more drinks over to the table, then took my seat again, waiting for her to do the same. Sera glanced back and forth between me and the other tables, then finally heaved a resigned sigh and sank down across from me, setting her tray on the table.

"Who do I speak with to have your company for the evening?"

Her head shot up. "I'm sorry?"

"Your company," I repeated. "I'd like to purchase your company for the evening."

She stared at me with wide eyes, her lips parted in surprise. "Oh. Uh..."

"Are you already booked?"

She didn't respond, just continued to stare at me like she couldn't comprehend what I was asking her.

"Let me speak to your manager. I'll pay twice your normal fee. I'm sure he or she won't have an issue with you canceling on your original date if you have one." This wasn't the reason I'd come here. I'd only planned to find her and get some answers. It shouldn't have taken me more than thirty minutes.

However, as soon as I saw her standing there in that outfit—the wet dream of every fucking pedophile within a hundred-mile radius—my plans abruptly changed. There was no way in fucking hell I was going to let her prance around looking like that.

Sera stuck the lollipop back into her mouth and stared at me.

I frowned. "What the fuck is wrong with you? I know you can speak intelligently." Was she fucking drugged? Did she self-medicate so she could do this kind of work? I knew some people felt the need to numb themselves that way, but were desperate enough for money they did whatever they had to do to get through it. I'd never hired those people. I preferred my partners to enjoy spending time with me. "Who is your manager?" I asked again.

Finally, she seemed to snap out of it. Pulling the candy out of her mouth, she laid it on the tray as a waiter set our drinks on the table and disappeared again. "I think you have the wrong idea, Enzo." She glanced down at her outfit and back at me. "I don't have a manager."

"That makes things easy, then. My offer stands. Go get your things."

"Enzo, I'm not for hire. I'm just a waitress."

I leaned forward and put my elbows on the table. "Then why did you come to my hotel room last weekend in that tacky fuck-me dress?"

"I told you, I was only filling in for Jade. It was just that one night," she emphasized. "I'm not an escort. Not yet, anyway."

I narrowed my eyes at that last part, and my voice was little more than a growl when I asked, "What do you mean 'not yet?'"

CHAPTER 7

Serafina

What the fuck was Enzo doing here? I'd come into work expecting the usual—a night of delivering drinks to the girls and their clients while dodging anyone who got too grabby. Most of the men who frequented the club tended to blur the line of who was for sale and who wasn't. When I first started, I was told it came with the job and to figure out a way to deal with it. Of course, the outfits they put us in didn't help matters. But it was what it was. So I would smile, dodge hands, collect my tips, ignore my aching feet in these fucking heels, and then go back to Jade's and fall into bed. Or couch, as the case may be.

I did not expect to see the man I'd barely escaped once sitting at one of my tables, sunglasses hiding his thoughts as he stared down at his phone. According to Jade, he'd only been here once, and that was the first time she'd met him for a date. She always met her clients here the first time, so she could see what their vibe was before she went anywhere alone with them. And even then, she was prepared with pepper spray and a weekly self-defense class. It was one of the main reasons I'd filled in for her on that particular date the other night. I wanted to lose my virginity and then never see the guy again.

So when Rob told me someone was asking about me when I went up to the bar to collect my next order and he'd given me this drink to deliver, I didn't think much of it. That was par for the course when I worked in a place like this dressed like a blow-up doll.

I stared at Enzo across the table. "Aren't you angry with me for not showing up the other night?" I had disrespected him, and that wasn't something that went over well with someone like him.

"Yes. Extremely."

Oh.

Suddenly, he stood up from the table.

I stood up, too, picking up my tray. "I'm sure one of the other girls would be happy to be your date tonight if Jade isn't available." As soon as the words were out of my mouth, I wished I could take them back. It struck me that I didn't want to see him with another woman. Shocked at the sudden appearance of *that* ugly emotion, I immediately tried to shut that shit down. I had no claim on this man. And I didn't want any. Honestly, he scared me a little. And I wasn't the only one who felt that way. I saw the looks he was getting from the other patrons. The guy radiated danger like a strong cologne.

"I don't want a date," he told me. "I just need to talk to you. I'll go let them know you're leaving."

My heart skipped a beat, stopped, then took off again, racing so fast I got light-headed.

Oh, fuck. He knows.

I didn't have to see his eyes to know this. "Oh." I needed time to figure out what I was going to say when he confronted me. "I get off at one if I'm not ordered to go clean out my locker before then. Can't we talk later? Tonight is usually a good tip night, and I really need the money."

He stared at me for a long moment as I tried to find his eyes behind the dark lenses. I couldn't tell if he was angry, or...what. Then he sat back down.

"What are you doing?"

"Waiting," he told me. "I'll take another whiskey, please."

Waiting. He was *waiting*. Fuck me. "Are you sure you don't have somewhere—"

"I'll wait, Sera. Another drink, please." He adjusted his jacket around him, crossed his legs, and leaned back in his chair with one arm on the table, his fingers tapping an impatient rhythm on the black tabletop.

"You already have two on the table."

He raised one eyebrow above the top of his sunglasses.

Not knowing what else to do or say, I pivoted on my excruciatingly high heel and marched back to the bar. "I need another whiskey," I told Rob.

He slid a double across the bar with a scowl. "Tell Mr. Delligatti it's on the house. As a matter of fact, all of his drinks tonight will be coming out of your paycheck."

"What?" I stood there, frozen, with one hand wrapped around the drink. "It was a fucking accident, Rob."

"Tell that to Tom," was his response. "You're lucky he wasn't here yet to see that. And that I'm willing to put in a good word for you by telling him how you graciously offered to take care of the customer's tab and how pleased he was with your...service. I suggest you give him *anything* he wants."

He had me backed into a corner. I needed this job. Mostly because the entire premise of this club was discretion. People didn't talk here. Not to exes. Not to cops. Not even to people like my father's goons who would come looking for me if they heard I was in Austin. So I could work here and make some money. Money that would enable me to get farther away. Maybe even disappear completely.

When I left my father's house, I'd had nothing but the clothes on my back and a suitcase full of essentials. I'd never been allowed to have my own bank account. Or my own friends. I was only allowed to get my driver's license and a car because I convinced my father in one of his weaker moments that I would make someone a better wife if I had a college degree, and it would be easier and less conspicuous to his enemies if I could just drive myself to class like any other college kid. It had taken some doing, but I finally managed to talk him into it. And I thanked god every day that I did. After I'd graduated and held my degree in my hands, my life went back to being cooped up in our house surrounded by guards, waiting for the day my father sold me to some old man so he could up his own rank within the family.

And during that entire time, I was the perfect daughter. I did as I was told. I went with him to functions filled with criminals and I smiled and kept my eyes down and my mouth shut so I didn't catch hell when we got home. I did as little as possible to call attention to myself, from my father or anyone else. It was the only way I'd known to stay alive.

But I knew it wouldn't last. With every birthday, I felt my father's eyes on me more and more often. At twenty-five, I was well beyond the usual marrying age for the daughter of a mafia man. We women were used as a gesture of good will, or sometimes bargaining chips to placate the men. Make them feel bigger than they were. More important. And the thought of becoming some gangster's trophy wife, of sleeping in the same bed with him and letting him rut over me every night, made me want to vomit. So one day, I just walked out of the house, got into my car, and left. No one stopped me. No one even thought to question me because I'd always been such a good girl who never caused any trouble.

I drove as far as I could go without any money to get gas, which was three hours away to Austin. I pulled up right outside of this club, walked in, and asked for a job. I'd only planned to stay long enough to get a paycheck, until I'd found out exactly what type of business it was and decided it was safe enough for me to stay for a while. And that's how I met Jade, who offered me a place to stay when she found out I was sleeping in my car and washing up in the restroom at the back of the club before my shift every night. I'd been at her place about two weeks when I asked her if I could take her place one night on one of her dates. If I got rid of this pesky virginity, I wouldn't be nearly as valuable if I was ever found and forced back into my father's home.

If I survived the beating he would give me for running off and "defiling" myself, maybe, just maybe, I'd be able to have some semblance of freedom. Or at the very least, have a say in who I ended up marrying.

It'd seemed like a good back-up plan at the time. However, after my scare the other night, I'd decided I would concentrate on saving money so I could leave this state as soon as possible. Losing my virginity along the way would be nothing but a bonus, but it would be by my choice. Not a decision forced on me by my situation. And not with someone who knew my father.

I took Enzo's drink and put it on my tray, along with a few others for the next table. Drinks that would also come out of my paycheck for making my customers wait while I "took a break to flirt" per Rob. I dropped those off first before taking Enzo's whiskey over to him. Setting it on the table, I turned to check on the rest of my tables.

"Why are you wearing that?"

His question caught me off guard. I turned back around. "What?"

Enzo ran his eyes up and down my body. And even though I was sufficiently covered, I felt naked and couldn't stop myself from looking down to make sure he hadn't singed the clothes from my body with nothing but his burning gaze. One I could feel even with the sunglasses acting as a barrier between us. I couldn't even imagine how scorched I would feel if they weren't there. "It's my uniform," I told him. "I wasn't really given much of a choice." Every waitress here was a different character. With my height, curves, pink hair, and piercings, I was a "naughty little girl." Sloane, the head server, picked the looks for us.

He took a sip of his whiskey and set the glass back on the table. "None of the other waitstaff are dressed up like a man's fantasy come to life."

I frowned down at him. "The other waitstaff here tonight are men." Their uniforms weren't as diverse. Just similar combinations of black slacks and shiny, silver shirts with black vests.

His phone vibrated on the table, and he picked it up from the table and turned his attention to the screen. Breathing a sigh of relief, I took advantage of the opportunity and went to check on the rest of my tables.

The rest of the night was uneventful, other than the fact that Enzo's eyes followed me everywhere I went. Even when I wasn't looking, I could feel his gaze on me. It burned along my skin everywhere his eyes touched until I felt like I was sunburned. And I didn't know if it was his presence or if the gentlemen in the club were just busy with other things, but they were much less handsy than normal tonight, and for that I was thankful. It wasn't unusual for me to find bruises on my skin in the mornings because someone was having a hell of a good time and grabbed me a little too forcefully as they tried to force me to join the party.

However, by the time I cashed in my tips and walked to the back to get my things out of my locker, my nerves were so on edge I wanted to jump out of my skin. So, when I heard his voice directly behind me, I bit back a scream just in time.

"Now can we talk?"

Spinning around, I slammed my back against the wall of lockers, trying to put some space between us, but he was having none of it. One of the handles dug into the back of my hip, but I ignored it. "What do you want, Enzo?" I asked, transferring all of the fear I felt into annoyance. Even though my feet were fucking killing me, I stood tall in my heels, glad I hadn't changed into my slip-on sneakers yet. At least with these ridiculous shoes on he didn't tower over me quite so much.

His nostrils flared as he inhaled deeply. He didn't answer me right away, and when he did, I was surprised by what he said. "Come with me back to the hotel."

"No." I didn't know how he was even standing straight. He'd just sat at my table for six straight hours and drank whiskey, not moving except to go to the bathroom a few times. And as ready as I'd been to hop into bed with him the other night, I wasn't so eager now that I knew who he was. I needed to stay away from him. Not get more intimate. But obviously he wasn't used to taking no for an answer.

"That wasn't a request, Sera." He paused, and I tried desperately to see his eyes to get an idea of what he was thinking. "Or should I call you Fina?"

My heart dropped into my stomach as I tried to keep my face straight. Fuck. Fuck. *Fuck!*

I was planning to change my name completely, but because "Serefina Cordaro" was on my license that I had to show to get this job, I went by Sera, hoping that would be enough to throw people off. "My name is Sera," I told him.

"Good," he said, surprising me. "I prefer Sera." He glanced over my shoulder at my closed locker. "Do you have everything you need?"

I swallowed hard and nodded, but my mind was racing, trying to think of a way I could get out of this predicament I'd made for myself. But all I could think of was to tell him the truth. "I don't want to go back to the hotel with you. If you want to talk, we can talk, but I'd prefer somewhere more public."

He cocked his head. "Smart girl. However, I don't want anyone to see us talking, so I must insist on somewhere more private. After all, I assume you don't want it getting back to your father that you're here." He raised one eyebrow, and I shook my head in confirmation. "And I don't think you'd want to find a table here, since it *is* your place of employment and someone might overhear us."

"No," I whispered. The people here didn't know where I came from, although it wouldn't be hard to find out. But I didn't think they really cared as long as I showed up to work and did my job. However, if someone overheard us and I was found out, they wouldn't be able to ignore it.

"So that leaves us with the hotel."

"But people there will see us come in together."

"The people there are paid well to stay out of my business. And they know what will happen to them if they don't."

Chills chased each other across my skin. He never raised his voice or changed his tone, yet I felt the cold fingers of death skim the back of my neck at his careless words.

Gently, he took the tote bag that held my things from me, set it down, and helped me into my coat. Then, with a hand on the small of my back, he ushered me out of the break room and to the back door of the club. The night air was chilly when we stepped outside, and I could smell rain. I shivered and wrapped my arms around myself.

He pointed with the hand holding the bag. "My car is right there."

A black SUV was parked just a few feet from the door. "I can follow you to the hotel," I told him, working hard to keep the panic out of my voice. "That way, you don't have to worry about bringing me back here for my car. Is it the same place you were staying before?"

He didn't bother to respond to my generous offer, and I took that as a no. Once we reached the SUV, Enzo helped me into the passenger seat and set the tote at my feet. But instead of closing the door, he opened my bag and started digging around inside. "Hey! That's my stuff!"

"Is this your stuff?" He held up an expensive lighter made of champagne gold and diamonds.

I felt my face burn, but I'd been so nervous all night I was honestly surprised that was the only thing that wound up in my tote. I didn't know how he saw me take it from the other table in my section when even the owner of the lighter didn't, but apparently, he had. "I grabbed it accidentally. I would've returned it to Lost and Found tomorrow when I came in."

He studied me a moment. "Stay here. I'll be right back." Closing the door, he walked back into the club.

I watched him go, one hand on the door handle. My car was parked off to the side of the lot. I had my keys. All I had to do was jump out and run to my car. I could be gone by the time he came back outside.

But what good would that do? He'd just come back tomorrow. And the day after. And the day after that, until I went with him. And maybe the next time, he wouldn't ask so nicely. So I might as well get it over with.

My eyes skittered around the interior. Same as last time, the vehicle looked like it had just come back from being detailed. I opened the center console, then the glove box. Both were empty. Nothing to identify the man who drove it.

I was still sitting there when he returned. If he noticed that I wanted nothing more than to bolt, he didn't mention it. Just started the engine and pulled away. We rode along in silence for about ten minutes before he said, "Is it money?"

Startled from my daydream of escape as I watched the city go by, I turned and studied his profile. "What?"

"The reason you steal. Is it because you need money?" He never took his eyes off the road. Behind his sunglasses, I caught a glimpse of long, dark lashes as we drove under a streetlight.

I didn't want to talk about my *affliction*, as I liked to call it. Not with him. "Is it because you're trying to hide something?" I countered. "Is that why you always wear those dark glasses?"

One corner of his mouth turned up. "Touché."

"You know, we could just talk right here in the car as we drive around," I continued. "There's no reason to drag me up to your hotel room." I was getting more and more nervous by the minute that he was leading me into a trap. Was someone waiting there to drag me back to my father? "Or we could stop and get a coffee somewhere or something."

"The only place open around here this late is Denny's, and their coffee tastes like shit."

I waited for him to say more, and wasn't surprised when he didn't. Tears filled my eyes. It looked like my taste of freedom was over before it ever really began. I wasn't too proud to beg, but I knew it wouldn't do me any good. I mean, just look at him. Even wearing a suit, I could tell this guy had a body that was hard and unforgiving, and he had a personality to match. Plus, he was mafia. He wouldn't care about my life or what was waiting for me when I got back. So I kept silent and wondered how badly I'd break my ankle in these heels if I jumped from the moving vehicle before we stopped.

As if he knew exactly what I was thinking, Enzo wrapped his fingers around my wrist and hung on as he turned the wheel one handed and pulled into the circle drive in front of the hotel. He didn't release me even when we stopped. Shifting the car into park, he took off his seatbelt and angled his body toward mine, ignoring the young girl outside waiting to park the car for him. A good-looking guy with blond hair opened my door with a smile, but closed it again when Enzo shook his head at him. "There's no one waiting upstairs," he told me. And again, I wondered if he could read minds or if I was just that fucking obvious. "It'll just be you and me. And I just want to talk. Okay?"

I didn't see where I had much of a choice. "Okay," I answered.

He released my wrist and opened his door, tossing his keys to the attendant before walking around the front of the car and saying something to the blond guy that sent him scurrying back to his stand by the entrance of the hotel as Enzo opened my door for me and helped me out, then he grabbed my tote from the floorboard and carried it inside for me.

I noticed the way he scanned the area around him constantly. He'd done the same thing at the club, always watching for trouble, and I wondered if he was even aware that he did it. All I could think of was how exhausting it must be to always be on alert like that. I supposed all mafia men lived that way, just waiting for someone to take them out for some imagined—or very real—slight. Or just to get them out of the way.

As he escorted me inside, my skin felt cold and clammy, and my lungs felt too tight to draw a full breath. Even though he'd told me I had nothing to worry about and I'd agreed to come with him, I couldn't help the sense of dread that came over me as we crossed the foyer with its high ceilings and white columns, my heels clicking on the marble floors a countdown to the demise of my freedom. And possibly my life.

CHAPTER 8

Enzo

I'd lied to her in the car just now. We could've had this conversation anywhere. I'd gone to the club to get answers, not to get under her ruffled skirt. But the moment I saw her in that baby doll dress, my plans had changed. I couldn't even bring myself to leave and come back when she got off, not when every fucking perv in the fucking place couldn't take their eyes off of her.

And I counted myself among them. This need I had to get Sera back up to my room overrode any common sense I had.

So I sat at her table all fucking night, waiting for someone to be stupid enough to lay so much as a finger on her ruffled ass as she served them and give me an excuse to take out some of these pent-up emotions on their face.

What the fuck was it with this woman? She was driving me utterly insane. And there was no reason for it. I'd fucked many women in my life. Women who were prettier, more worldly, and who did whatever the fuck I told them without arguing with me. I didn't need this...distraction in my life.

And yet, now that I had her all to myself, I didn't want to let her leave.

I locked the door and unbuttoned my jacket, leaving her standing just inside as she looked around with wide eyes. Leaving my jacket lying on the couch in the sitting area as I walked past, I took off my watch and laid it on the nightstand by the bed, then unbuttoned and rolled up my sleeves. I left my gun holstered to my side. I was more comfortable with it on me in case something happened. Unless I was fucking or sleeping. Then I kept it on the nightstand within easy reach. Leaving my sunglasses on, I went to the small bar and poured myself another whiskey. "Drink?" I asked her.

She was still in her coat, standing by the door. "Do you have any wine?"

"I have whiskey," I told her.

"That'll work," she said.

I poured her a glass and added a large cube of ice, as she didn't seem the type to drink it straight. Indicating for her to join me in the sitting room, I waited for her to sit down before handing her the drink and took a seat in the corner, angling my body toward hers and resting one arm on the back of the couch. She sat as far away from me as she could on the edge of the cushion, her knees pressed together like a virgin on her first date. She wouldn't look at me. Instead, she stared down at the coffee table. Her hand shook as she lifted the glass to her lips and took a cautious sip, coughing a little as the alcohol burned a trail down her throat. I allowed her two more sips, and then I demanded answers.

"You *are* Serafina Cordaro, daughter of Ciro Cordaro, correct?"

She gave me a quick glance, taking another sip of her drink to bolster her courage before she answered me. "I am."

I was impressed. She didn't even try to lie her way out of it. "Your father is looking for you."

"I assumed he would be."

"Why did you run away from home?"

At first, I thought she wasn't going to answer. But then she turned to look at me, curiosity in her eyes as she said, "Would you enjoy spending your life locked up in your room waiting for your father to marry you off to some old, crusty Italian so you can live a life no better than livestock, there to breed his offspring and take whatever he gives you while being expected to smile and laugh and act like you have a wonderful life when he deigns to take you somewhere?" She stopped and took a breath. "Because I don't."

"I think you're exaggerating."

"I'm not." She took another drink.

I got up to refill her glass. "From what I understand, you were allowed to go to college. That leads me to believe you led a somewhat normal life."

"I was only allowed to get my degree because I managed to convince my father it would make me more of an asset as a wife if I had a head for business. And it took me three years to talk him into it."

That didn't surprise me. I'd only met her father in person once before. He had an over bloated ego and a penchant for underage girls. Not a very paternal man. "What about your mother? She must miss you." I handed her refilled glass back to her and resumed my seat.

"My mother is dead." Her voice was flat as she imparted that news, and she didn't give me any other details. But something about the way she said it...

I put that away for later.

"Are you going to call him?" Wide blue-gray eyes clashed with mine, still hidden behind my glasses. "Have you already?"

I shook my head and twirled the liquid in my glass, watching as the light played off the amber hues. "I haven't called anyone. Nor have I told anyone that I saw you."

She seemed surprised. "Why not?"

"Why should I?" I countered. "What will I get out of sending you back to your father?" I paused, an idea forming in my head. Although if I were to be honest with myself, it'd been forming since the moment Luca handed me her photo. "Whereas I think I could get something much more valuable by agreeing to stay silent."

Her spine stiffened. "What do you want?"

Ah, so she was intelligent. Something I already knew.

"I don't have any money," she told me. "I left there with nothing."

"I have no use for your money."

Her eyes darkened knowingly as she stared at me, and she spoke her next question as though she already knew the answer. "Then what do you want?"

"I want you."

"I'm not for sale," she answered immediately.

"You were the other night."

"That was before I knew who you were."

Never taking my eyes from hers, I took a long drink, then balanced my glass on my thigh, one finger rubbing along the rim, my other arm along the back of the couch. "I'll pay you well for the pleasure of your company, Sera. Enough so you can keep running if you want. Once I'm done with you, of course. And in return, I promise to keep my mouth shut about your whereabouts. No one will know you're here in Austin or that I'd ever laid eyes on you."

She studied me with a puzzled expression, her bright eyes searching my face, searching for an ulterior motive. "Why the hell would you do that?"

"I think it's a fair exchange."

"No. I mean, why do you pay for sex? I would think you could have any woman—or man—you wanted just by walking into a room with your"—she waved a hand in the air, encompassing me in my entirety—"aura of looks, money, and danger. Why go through all of this?" She waved that same hand back and forth between us.

"Because I don't want someone I could pick up in a bar. I want you."

She smirked. "Well, technically, you just picked me up in a bar."

I chuckled, surprising both of us. "Again, touché."

Suddenly serious again, she asked, "And if I refuse your offer?"

"Then I'll put you back in the car and hand deliver you to your father's men right now." It was a lie. I would do no such thing. But I wasn't above telling her whatever I needed to in order to get her to agree to my offer. I didn't stop and rationalize why I was doing this. I didn't want to know the answer.

She stood up and walked over to the bar to refill her drink. I noticed her wince, and I tensed, wondering if something had happened to her tonight that I'd somehow missed before I realized it was from her shoes. I relaxed back against the couch cushions and watched her as she thought about my offer.

After a few moments, she turned back to me. "I'm sorry. I'm going to have to refuse your generous offer." Her tone led me to believe she thought it was anything but generous. But her eyes...her eyes showed me how horrified she was at the thought of going back to her father.

"I meant what I said," I told her. "You'll be back home locked in your room by sunup."

"I understand," she told me.

I wasn't expecting her to refuse me. Fucking again.

This wasn't acceptable.

Finishing her drink, she put her empty glass on the bar and walked over to the door, where she stood demurely and waited for me.

I studied her, noticing the tension in her jaw and the way she laced her fingers together in front of her to hide their trembling. She wouldn't look at me, but I could see the tight way she held her mouth. Was she bluffing? Or was she more afraid of me than her father?

Slamming my glass down on the table so hard it shattered, I stalked over to her, ignoring the blood running down my fingers and the way my heart wanted to pound out of my chest. She wasn't leaving me tonight. I wouldn't allow it.

She backed up fast when she saw me coming, almost tripping when one of her heels snagged the expensive carpet. When she hit the door, she twisted around and grabbed the door handle and pulled, but it was locked. I was on her before she could unlock it and get it open, spinning her back around and shoving her shoulders back against the door. I blocked her in with a hand on either side of her head. I didn't touch her, but I could feel her fear vibrating the air between us. "Where the fuck do you think you're going?"

"To the car," she squeaked.

"No," I told her. "You're staying here. With me."

"I don't want to," she whispered.

"Why the fuck not?"

"Because you scare me!" The words fell over themselves as they rushed out of her mouth.

They didn't turn me off.

They made my fucking cock hard as a goddamned rock.

I stared down at her. Her eyes were wide and lined with false eyelashes and glitter. Her lips were pink and glossy. And the silver hoop in her left nostril glinted in the light. With her pink hair and porcelain skin, she looked as sweet and innocent as the lollipop she was sucking on earlier. I wanted to taste her. I wanted those bright eyes on mine as I shoved my cock down her throat. I wanted to hurt her. To break her. To make her beg. I wanted to make her mine. My very own little doll to do with what I would.

"I scare you?" I asked.

She kept her face turned away and wouldn't look at me. "Yes," she whispered.

"More than your father?"

She didn't even hesitate. "Yes."

Cupping the side of her face in one hand, I turned her head until she was forced to look at me, leaving streaks of blood on her skin. "You should be scared of me, Sera. You should be fucking terrified." Not because I would hurt her, not like her father would. But because once she was mine, I knew I wouldn't be able to give her up. It was the real reason I paid for the company of whores. They were something I borrowed, like a library book. They were not to be owned. But Sera...

She stared at me with pleading eyes. "Enzo, please. Just let me go."

"It's way too late for that, baby girl." Her soft lips beckoned, and I rubbed the pad of my thumb over her plump lower lip, smearing my blood into the gloss until it darkened it to red. I watched with something akin to fascination as tears filled her eyes, and I saw myself swimming in their depths.

Reaching up, I removed my sunglasses.

Sera froze as she stared into my eyes for the first time. I knew what she was seeing. Anger. Determination. Lust. Desperation. Fear. Things I wished I could hide because knowing she could see these things within me made me feel vulnerable. Exposed. With a growl of frustration and need, I lowered my head and took her mouth with mine, tasting the salty copper of my blood on my tongue as I forced it between her lips. Moving my hand from her face to her throat, I held her against the door as I took what I needed from her, swallowing the little noises of protest she made. I'd offered her a way to come to me of her own free will as she'd done once before, but she chose to refuse me.

That was her choice.

And this was mine.

She tried to push me off, and I slowly tightened my grip, cutting off her air supply until she stopped fighting me. I moaned when she went still beneath me, taking my time as I tasted her, the tip of my tongue curling to play with the gap between her teeth before I filled her sweet mouth again, just like I would fill her pussy that I knew would be just as sweet.

Her teeth bit into my lower lip and I tasted more blood as I jerked back in surprise with a curse, losing my grip on her. Sera suddenly dropped down in front of me and I automatically took a step back, giving her room to bolt to the side and run into the room. As she did, she grabbed my gun from its holster. By the time I turned around, she was in the middle of the room with her feet braced apart and my gun pointed at the center of my chest. "What the fuck are you doing, Sera?"

"You need to let me leave," she said. Her voice was hoarse from the grip I'd had on her throat. "I want to leave."

Hands low on my hips, I watched her, taking in all of her tells. Her throat was red from my hand and her chest and cheeks were flushed. From anger? Adrenaline? Or lust? "What are you going to do if I don't? Are you going to shoot me?"

"Yes," she told me. But the tremor in her voice and the unsteady hold she had on the weapon told me a different story.

"No. You won't."

"I will," she insisted. "Let me leave, Enzo."

A little girl in pigtails was threatening me with my own weapon. I smiled, enjoying the way her eyes widened when she saw it. Slowly, I advanced on her. "Put the gun down, Sera."

"No."

I tilted my head to one side and saw that she had, indeed, taken the safety off. And her finger was on the trigger. Perhaps she wasn't as new at this as I first thought. It made sense if she was the daughter of a man in the mafia. "Did your father teach you to shoot?" I asked as I paced slowly back and forth in front of her so she would have to keep adjusting her aim. While I walked, I unrolled my sleeves, inching my way closer.

She barked out a laugh, but it was an ugly sound. "No," she said.

I waited for more information, but she didn't seem willing to give it to me. "Who taught you to shoot?"

"No one you would know," was her only answer.

"So I guess your father wasn't quite as strict as you let on." I wanted to keep her talking. Keep her distracted. Until I could get close enough to get the gun away from her.

"I didn't get locked down until I got to childbearing age," she clarified.

Which told me she hadn't handled a weapon for quite a few years. It explained how she seemed to know what she was doing and yet lacked the confidence needed to actually pull the trigger. I was only about two feet from the weapon now. All I had to do was wait for the exact moment her arms were a second behind my movements and I could grab her wrists and pull her forward while I twisted around until my back was to her. Then I could get the weapon away from her without getting shot.

"Sera." I picked up my pace just slightly.

"What?" she gritted out.

"Don't make me hurt you." Those were my last words before I rushed her. Two seconds later, the gun was in my hands, and she was backing toward the bedroom with her hands held out in front of her.

"I'm sorry," she told me. Her voice was thick with tears. "I just want to leave. Do what you think you need to, Enzo. But please, just give me a head start. That's all I ask."

"I've already told you. It's too late for that. The choice I gave you was just me being nice." She'd been mine since the moment I first opened the door and saw her standing on the other side. She was always meant to be mine.

Alessandra's face floated before me, her eyes accusing. I shook my head, chasing it away. This wasn't the same. I'd loved Alessandra with everything in me. And that love had cost me the lives of my wife and son. Sera was just a passing fascination. I'd tire of her just like I'd tired of every other woman I'd been with. Nothing would happen to her. She'd go back to her father and live the life of a mafia wife with someone else.

I emptied the clip and set both that and the gun on the table behind me beside my watch, not taking my eyes from her the entire time. The backs of her knees hit the bed, and she glanced over her shoulder to see what had stopped her retreat.

Perfect.

Just where I wanted her.

CHAPTER 9

Serafina

My body went hot and cold as he prowled toward me like some kind of beautiful nightmare. His dark eyes were focused in on mine, and they burned with so many emotions I didn't know how he kept from spontaneously combusting. I saw now why he hid behind those dark glasses. Everything he felt—every want, every need, every fear, every raw desire—showed themselves in those eyes. They hid nothing from me. Internally, he was on fire. And what he burned for right now was *me*.

And it both excited and terrified me all at once.

I didn't know if it was all the whiskey he'd had that night or if he was always like this, but I tried again to get through to him. "Enzo, please. Don't do this." How I'd ever thought it was a good idea to give my virginity to this man, I didn't know. I was terrified of unleashing all of that burning energy inside of him on my innocent body. And I was afraid to tell him how innocent I actually was for fear that it would only excite him more. "Please. Let's talk about this. I'm sure we can work something out."

"We're done talking, Sera. I made you an offer."

"One I didn't accept."

He stopped so close to me that if I took a deep breath, my breasts would touch his chest, but there was nowhere else for me to go. I swallowed hard as his eyes traveled over my face, from my hairline to my chin, before they finally narrowed on mine. "It's the only offer you're going to receive from me. And it wasn't really up for debate."

"That's not an offer at all if you won't accept my decision not to take it. It's a demand. Which makes you no better than my father." I took shallow breaths, trying to ignore the way his scent surrounded me. He smelled like trees under the moon, cloaked by mist. My pulse raced, making me lightheaded, and nerves fluttered in my stomach.

But other things were happening lower.

I flinched when he raised his hand toward me, but he only wrapped one of my pigtails around his fingers. "Such a sweet little thing," he murmured. "Ever since I first saw you, I've imagined what you would look like on your knees, this perfect mouth stuffed with my cock. I can't stop thinking about it."

"Enzo, please." I kept my voice low and quiet, hoping to calm the beast within him. "Don't do this."

His eyes traveled over my face, and I thought for a moment that I was getting through to him. But then he wrapped his other hand in my hair and forced my head down until I had no choice but to sit on the bed. It was that, or have my face scrape down the front of his shirt and pants. Once I was sitting, he released my hair and removed his shirt, revealing powerful shoulders and arms, with tattoos on the left side over his pec and shoulder and down his arm. My eyes wandered along slabs of hard muscle that rippled down his flat stomach to the "V" that dipped between his hips. Then he undid his slacks, pushing them down his hips, along with his black boxer briefs until his long, thick cock was free. A thick vein ran along the underside, and I had the sudden urge to run my tongue along it until I reached the swollen, purplish head.

His hands were gentle as they smoothed my hair and cupped my cheeks. "I can't get you out of my fucking head, Sera. Trust me, I've tried."

A surprising shock of jealousy whipped through me, heating my blood. What did that mean? He tried? How? With who? I had my answer with his next words.

"Do you know how many times a day I find myself locked in a bathroom fucking my fist until my cock is raw because all I can see is you in that fucking excuse for a dress you wore when you showed up at my door?" He laughed, but it was an ugly sound. "But this shit you're wearing tonight...yeah...you just gave me a new fucking fantasy to obsess over." He paused, and I could feel the weight of tension around us. Electric currents pulling us together even as we both tried to fight it. "I gotta get you out of my system, baby girl. You're too distracting. And it's dangerous for me to be distracted. Not just for me, but for the man I work for."

He gripped himself in his one hand, breathing hard as he slid his fist up and down its thick length. My lips parted as I watched. I couldn't seem to get enough air.

"Get on your knees and put me in your mouth, Sera."

A tear slid down my cheek even as the deep muscles of my womb tightened and released, sending a rush of moisture between my thighs. I wasn't completely ignorant about sex. In this day and age, it would be ridiculous for anyone to make it into their mid-twenties without exploring that side of themselves. I saw movies. I had the internet. I'd explored myself in the darkness of my bedroom at night. But I'd never had the opportunity to be this intimate with another person.

It was...intoxicating.

I slid off the bed and landed on my knees in front of him. Despite my body's reaction to what he was doing, I didn't want to do this. Not because I wasn't attracted to him. I mean, fucking look at him. But because he wasn't giving me a choice. However, I was afraid of what he would do if I kept refusing him. Would he hit me? Rape me? Jade told me he'd never done those things to her. But she'd also never told him no.

I turned my face away. This was not the way I ever imagined my first sexual experience would go. And maybe I was naive and making more of the situation than what it was, but if he wanted me to suck him off, he would have to put that gun to my head.

"Put me in your mouth, Sera," he growled.

I kept my eyes averted and shook my head, silent tears sliding freely down my cheeks as I struggled with what I knew was right and what my body craved. My back began to ache from holding myself so stiff as I waited to see what he would do next.

Seconds ticked by, and I could sense his own inner struggle. Then, with a sound like something I imagined an animal would make, his free hand wrapped itself in my hair and he forcefully turned my head until the head of his cock rubbed my lips. I kept them pressed shut, refusing to take him into my mouth as he stroked himself.

"Eyes up here," he ordered. His voice was low and strained. When I didn't immediately comply, he tightened his grip in my hair until I winced from the pain and opened my eyes.

As soon as they met his, he bared his teeth in a snarl and his fist started pumping his cock faster. I watched, fascinated by the waves of pleasure and pain and...was that shame?...that burned within them. I saw his frustration. His fury that I wouldn't do what he wanted. What he needed. His breaths came faster and harder, his mouth falling open and his chest heaving. The tribal tattoos covering his left pec and shoulder seeming to writhe across his skin as the muscle underneath tensed and released with his grip on my hair.

And the entire time, he held my eyes with his, drawing me into the act whether I wanted to be there or not. My nipples hardened and rubbed against the material of my dress, and there was an ache between my thighs, somewhere between pleasure and pain, that made me want to squeeze them together. I kept my hands fisted at my sides, refusing to touch myself, even though it nearly killed me.

I felt moisture on my lips, and without thinking about it, I licked it away, tasting the musky saltiness of the pre-cum dripping from the slit at the tip of his cock. I moaned when it coated my tongue, wanting to taste more of him despite my own stubborn refusal to do so.

Enzo clenched his jaw so hard muscles popped out at the hinge, the fire in his eyes searing my very soul as he slid his fist faster and faster up and down the length of his cock. The head jabbed me in the mouth as he rocked his hips and pulled my head forward as if I was sucking him.

Unable to take the intensity of his gaze any longer, I dropped my eyes just in time to see his stomach muscles tighten and release repeatedly as my name escaped his lips. A second later, I shut them tight as something warm, thick, and wet hit me in the face, covering my mouth and chin to run down my neck and drip down my chest into my cleavage.

When it was done, I thought he would release his grip on my hair, but he didn't. Instead, he held my head still as he smeared his cum across my closed lips with his fingers. Then he pushed his thumb between my lips until he pressed against my teeth, forcing me to taste him again. He rubbed it into the skin of my jaw, my throat, and across my chest, dipping his fingers into my cleavage before bringing them back up to my lips.

"You're mine, Sera." The words were whispered, and there was a slight tremor to his voice, almost like he was afraid if he said them too loud I would up and disappear right out from in front of him.

He let go of my hair, and I blinked my eyes open, staring at his hands as he zipped himself back up into his pants. He went into the bathroom and came out a few seconds later with a fluffy white hand towel.

I hadn't moved. I was still on my knees beside the bed with my hands clenched into fists and my back screaming from fighting him. Enzo kneeled in front of me and gently wiped away what semen remained on my skin. I wouldn't look at him. I couldn't. I couldn't even cry anymore. I was horrified at what just happened. Embarrassed. And in some weird kind of post-traumatic numbness or something. But in the back of my mind, I felt how wet I was and how sensitive my nipples were, aching for him to touch me. I've never had a man react like this toward me, and I didn't know how to handle it. Nothing in my life had prepared me to be the recipient of such raw, animalistic need.

"I want to go home," I whispered when I found my voice, still keeping my eyes down. My face was on fire. I needed to be alone so I could process what just happened and how I felt about it, because while a part of me was embarrassed and disgusted and felt used, another part of me was more turned on then I've ever been in my life. If he asked me right now to strip and lie on the bed so he could lick me all over, I honestly didn't know that I would have the willpower to keep fighting him.

He rubbed his hand gently over the top of my head, smoothing my hair as I felt his eyes search my face. "Sera...I..." He paused. "There's no need to feel ashamed." When I didn't respond, he helped me to my feet and held out his hand. "Come on."

I allowed him to help me up, my mind racing. Was he going to let me leave? Or was he going to lock me up in this hotel room?

Instead of taking me out of the room, he sat me on the bed. And as he turned to sit beside me, I could see that he was still hard. Quickly, I averted my eyes, staring down at the navy-blue carpet.

"I would like you to listen to the terms of my offer," he told me. "Sera. Look at me."

Slowly, I turned my head and met his gaze.

His brown eyes had lost a little of their fire, but not all of it. He still looked at me like he was a starving man. Like he owned me now. "You're in my blood. And even after what happened here tonight, I want more. I want you to be mine, and only mine, until we can get...whatever the fuck this is...out of our system."

"What if I don't want you?"

One side of his mouth lifted in a hint of a smirk. "Am I ugly to you?"

I wanted to lie and say yes, but I couldn't. Not with him looking straight through me the way he was. "No," I told him.

"Are you attracted to me physically?"

I knew what my body had felt when I was on my knees in front of him, even as waves of humiliation surged through me. "Yes," I told him honestly. "Or at least I was before tonight." I couldn't resist adding that little dig at his behavior, even though I didn't know why I would've expected anything more from him. From what I'd heard, he was a made man. Not born into this life. He'd had to work harder, fight harder, to get where he was. And as I knew well, mafia men took what they wanted with little thought to the consequences of their actions. Why would he be any exception?

I wasn't expecting him to own up to what he'd done, but again, he surprised me. "I told you, I couldn't get you out of my fucking head, Sera." He sounded angry, but I wasn't sure if it was at me or at himself.

It wasn't anywhere near an apology, but it was probably as close as I was going to get.

His tone had gentled again when he said, "I'm not always a gentleman, Sera. But I swear you'll be safe with me. No one will hurt you while I'm around to protect you." He waited a moment for me to take that in. "I know you stand up for yourself. It's gotten you this far, and I respect that about you even as it drives me completely insane. But you don't really want to go back to your father, do you? So he can marry you off to some *stronzo* who'll parade you around in front of his friends and beat you when you don't have dinner ready on time?"

I shook my head. "No," I admitted, finally bringing myself to look at him. "I really don't. But I also don't want to trade one prison for another. You can't just throw money at me and expect me to have sex with you."

"Why not? That's what you were here for the other night, were you not?"

Yes, that's exactly why I'd been there, but still... "That was different."

"Why?"

Why? "Because it was my choice to be here."

Reaching over, he took one of my hands in his and brought it over to his lap where he rested our joined hands on his thigh. "Alright," he said. "I'll give you the choice. So, here is my offer. If you agree to stay with me, I won't tell anyone that you're here. Not even my closest friends. I'll keep you safe. And, when things have run their course between us, I'll give you the money to go wherever you want and start a brand-new life. I'll help you change your name, buy you anything you need, and you can forget all about me and your father and everyone else in this world if you want."

Like any offer, this one sounded too good to be true. I had to ask, "And what exactly do I have to do in return? Will I be locked in this room for you to use whenever you want?"

His eyes narrowed in warning. "You won't be locked in this room unless you force me to do so. I'd like this to be an agreement between us, Sera. You'll be allowed to live your life, as long as you are careful. You can continue to work at the club if you'd like. You can have your friends. You can even stay wherever you're living like you've been doing because I can't always be here at night, and no one would think to look for you there. However"—his eyes clashed with mine—"on the other side of it, you will make yourself available to me whenever you're not working. I'll expect you to answer your phone when I call. I don't care where you are or what you're doing. And I'll give you a burner phone to use when you talk to me. And when I summon you here, or anywhere, you come without question. And you won't pursue the escort business. I do *not* share, Sera."

No, he was too possessive. I could tell that already. And it raised a lot of red flags. "And what will you do with me while I'm with you?"

"Whatever the fuck I want to," he said darkly. "But I promise you, it'll be pleasurable for you, too. If you allow it to be. I won't beat you or sell you out to other men. As a matter of fact, I have no qualms about cutting off the hands of any man who dares to touch you, with or without your permission."

I wasn't even shocked by that statement. Not because I didn't believe him, I did. But because even locked in my father's home, I overheard things. I knew how men like Enzo worked. "And for how long will I need to do this?" I thought this was a pertinent question. He still frightened me, but I could also see the honesty of what he said in his eyes. And if he truly meant what he was telling me, it didn't sound like the worst arrangement in the world. Especially if it would get me out of the reach of my father. Enzo would tire of me sooner or later, and then I would be free.

I thought I detected a pause, but then he said, "As long as it takes."

"For what? For you to rape me every night?"

Enzo cocked his head, then shoved his hand under my dress and cupped my pussy over my ruffled panties as I tried to push him away. "I can feel how wet you are, Sera. I saw you squirming for my touch even as you held yourself so fucking stiff while you watched me get off. I heard the sounds you made when you tasted my come. Don't try to pretend that you're not aching to have my cock inside of you."

He was right. There was no use lying about it while my legs were spreading apart of their own accord to give him more room to maneuver. But instead of giving me what I needed, he gave me a squeeze and pulled his hand away.

I clenched the bedspread and tried to slow my breathing. Fine. But just to knock him down a few pegs, I asked, "And what if, *after*, we..." I couldn't bring myself to say the words. "I decide I don't want to continue with this agreement."

I watched, fascinated, as the corners of his mouth turned up and creases formed along his cheeks, revealing strong white teeth and crinkles around the corners of his eyes. His smile took the breath from my lungs and made my heart pound.

"That won't happen," he told me.

I scowled at his oversized ego. "You seem pretty damn sure of yourself."

"I'm good at what I do. At *everything* I do. You won't regret allowing me to fuck you, Sera."

My eyes wandered over to the gun on the nightstand and I mentally counted how long it would take me to grab it and insert the clip, but I quickly discarded the idea. And not just because I knew I wouldn't be able to get to it before him, but because I felt strangely guilty for having the idea to begin with.

Tearing my eyes away from the weapon, I looked back over at Enzo to find him watching me, his expression completely blank even though he had to know what I'd just been thinking.

"So, what do you say?" he asked. "Do we have an agreement?"

My mind raced. I didn't want to agree with this. Making a deal with Enzo felt like I was turning over my body to the devil himself. But it wasn't like he was giving me a choice. It was either play along with him on his terms and have a little freedom or be locked in this room. Because let's be honest here, sending me back to my father wasn't really even on the table, no matter what he said. For whatever reason, Enzo wanted me for himself, and when it was done, I would be rid of my virginity, and I'd have money to start over wherever I wanted to go.

There was really only one answer I could give here. But first, because I was a practical girl, I had a question. "How much money are we talking about, exactly?"

CHAPTER 10

Enzo

Much as I hated to leave her, I needed to get back to Luca's. But I couldn't get Sera out of my head as I drove out to his lake house after dropping her off back at the club so she could get her car. Coming all over her face hadn't done anything to ease the hunger inside of me. If anything, it only made it worse.

I'd watched her walk away in that little baby doll dress, every cell in my body screaming at me to go after her and bring her back. To lock her away somewhere where no one else would see her dressed like that. Where they couldn't take her from me. But somewhere in the back of my mind, I knew that Sera would never accept being in a cage. She wasn't like Veda. She wouldn't understand. And she would never be happy living her life in a prison again, no matter how luxurious I made it for her.

No. If I didn't want to lose her, I had to let her have a taste of freedom. For a while, at least. Until she was too attached to me to leave.

No. This is wrong. You should send her back to her father. Or better yet, just give her the money and let her run. Away from you and this life.

I concentrated on the road in front of me, pushing away my conscience.

After some minor haggling over money I didn't give two shits about, she'd finally accepted my offer. Sera was completely and utterly mine to do with as I wanted for as long as it was mutually acceptable to both of us. She'd insisted on the "mutual" part, and I'd let her have it since it seemed to make her feel better about the whole deal. It wouldn't make much difference anyway. I'd seen the way she'd looked at me. Felt the way she'd responded to me when I'd forced my cock against her mouth. Heard the little moans she'd tried to stifle. She wasn't immune to me. She'd even admitted as much. She felt the pull between us as much as I did. And now she was mine until I decided otherwise.

And if anything happened to me, I would make sure she had a sizable amount of cash. Enough that she could change her identity and fly herself anywhere in the world and live in the lap of luxury for five years or more before she'd have to worry about figuring out a way to support herself. Longer if she lived more modestly. I'd call my lawyer and make the arrangements tomorrow.

You had to have Alessandra, and look what happened to her.

But Sera isn't Alessandra. She was born into this life.

And she still hates it.

I squeezed my eyes shut tight and tried to shake the thoughts from my head before refocusing on the road in front of me. I knew she didn't deserve this. But the very idea of allowing her to walk away from me had anxiety twisting my guts even as bright red fury tinged the edges of my vision. My hands tightened even more. I needed to get a grip on myself. This was fucking crazy. Even for me. Especially for me. I knew how I was, and I knew how to control this thing inside of me. I didn't date. I only used escorts. I didn't allow myself to become obsessed.

Yet, I barely knew the girl, and she was already in my blood. I shook my head. I should have just given her back to her father. Keeping her around like this wasn't healthy for me. The moment I'd opened that door and saw her face, that face that stole my breath from my lungs, I should've sent her on her way and slammed it closed again. But I didn't. Instead, I invited her into my space. I allowed her smile to brighten my world. Her voice to soothe me. Her body to enflame mine until the urge to see her sweet lips wrapped around my cock was something I couldn't control, and I forced her on her knees...

I wiped my hand over my mouth and ignored the hard on it gave me to think about how she still refused me until I ended up fucking my own hand anyway. But if she wanted to play, I was more than happy to show her the rules.

A hollow feeling opened up in my gut. She would never be safe from me now.

Out of habit, I went to look at my watch to check the time. The watch I no longer had because Sera had stolen it from my nightstand before we left, and this time I didn't catch her. Of course, I wasn't expecting her to steal from me, and I didn't even realize it was gone until after I dropped her off and I noticed it wasn't on my wrist.

Pulling up my contact list on the screen on my dash, I called the owner of the club where she worked. It was time to call in that favor he owed me from the time I found his teenage son being groomed by one of the family. I'd gotten him out of there and taken him the fuck home where he belonged. Mostly because he wasn't cut out for this life. The kid would've died before he hit twenty. His father, however, was forever grateful to me when I returned him to the family fold. Skip ahead five years later, and I'd run into the same guy at the club where Jade and Sera now worked. I didn't even remember the guy's name, but I did have his number under the name of the club. "It's me," I told him when he answered the phone.

"Enzo! What can I do for you?"

He was pushing the enthusiasm a little too hard, but I chose to ignore it. "You have a new girl working there. Pink hair. A nose ring. Wears the baby doll outfit."

"Yes. That would be Sera. Did she do something wrong?" He didn't even pause before he told me, "I'll get rid of her right away."

I rolled my eyes as I heard him rustling paper around like he was doing it that very minute. "No. That's not why I'm calling."

"Oh. Uh. Alright. Is there some other issue with her?"

"There is. Sera is now under my protection." I paused for effect. "Do you get my meaning, my friend? I want extra security on the nights she's working, and I want a guard waiting outside for her when she arrives for work. I also want a guard to walk her to her car at the end of her shift."

"I will check her schedule first thing tomorrow and get that set up," he assured me. No questions asked.

"And the most important thing. Are you listening?"

"Yes, yes, of course."

"No one—and I mean *no fucking one*—is to touch her. Sera is not for sale. She is under my protection," I repeated. "She can wait on tables because it makes her happy to feel like she has a job, but that's all she will do. If you fail to do any of these things, you will have to answer to me."

"I completely understand."

"Good." I hung up the phone. I didn't need to go into more detail. His club was in our territory, which meant we were the ones who made sure no one fucked with him. He knew exactly who I was, and he knew exactly what I meant when I said she was under my protection. Sera was now mine. And any harm that befell her while under his watch would cause his life to be cut violently short. It was the best I could do without assigning some of our own guards to keep an eye on her. And I couldn't do that without questions being raised, or worse, risking that someone might recognize her and go over my head to report her whereabouts to her father. At that point, there wouldn't be much I could do except beg Luca to kill his guard and keep my secret. And that wasn't something I wanted to put on him.

I arrived back at the lake house just in time to relieve Tristan.

He was at his station by the front door when I walked in. "Luca wants to see you," he told me.

"About?" I asked. Fear gripped my stomach that he'd already found out about Sera somehow and she would be taken from me before we ever had a chance.

Tristan shrugged. "Probably putting you on the missing person deal. I have to go deal with one of the capos."

"Which one?"

"Gino. His boy Salvatore is having a hard time controlling his impulses, and he's going to cause some major problems if we don't get him under control."

"What's he doing?"

"He shot one of the Irish in the back. No one is sure what happened or why."

I cursed softly under my breath. Things with the Irish had been a little touchy lately thanks to Luigi, Luca's father, and his fucking delusional decisions that Luca had to maneuver through as best he could without causing a war until he could take over his position as boss. "Is he dead?"

"No. Luckily, his brother, Gil, saw him pull his gun and tried to stop him. Missed the guy's head by inches and the bullet skimmed the side of his neck just beneath his jaw, from what I understand."

"Jesus Christ. What the fuck is the matter with that *stronzo?*"

"That's what Luca is sending me to find out. I'll be hanging out with Gino and the family for a while, so you'll need to handle everything here."

God fucking dammit. "Of course. Do whatever you need to do. And be careful."

He gave me a partial smile that didn't reach his eyes. "Will you let Luca know I'm heading over there? I'll watch the house tonight and talk to Gino in the morning."

I nodded and told him again to be careful, then locked the door behind him and checked the security system to make sure it was armed for the night before I found Luca in the kitchen with Veda.

"Hey, Enzo," she greeted me.

"Veda. How are you?"

She smiled. "Good. Thanks. I have a test tomorrow morning though, so I'd better go do some last-minute studying and let you guys talk."

"Good luck," I told her as she rose and took her teacup to the sink, then returned to give Luca a kiss before she left. She patted my arm as she passed, and I felt a surge of affection for this woman who had made my lifelong friend so happy. She also kept him on his toes, and I admired her for that also.

"I'll be up soon, *amore*," Luca called after her.

She smiled at him over her shoulder and went up the stairs.

He watched her until she was out of sight, a possessive look in his eyes. Then he sighed. "Enzo," Luca said. "Come sit with me."

I did as he asked, unbuttoning my coat, and taking a seat on the chair to his left. I took off my sunglasses and laid them on the table as I waited to hear what he had to say.

"What's going on with you, my friend?"

My immediate instinct was to take a deep breath and tell him everything. Luca was my oldest friend. No. He was more than that. He was family. He understood me as no one else did, except maybe Tristan. And yet, I hesitated. "What do you mean?"

"I had the security footage from the club sent over to me. There was no attempted break-in."

A reckless anger flared inside of me before I could control the impulse. "You didn't trust me? Didn't believe what I told you?"

"No," he told me honestly. "I didn't. Something is off with you, and I want to know what it is." When I didn't respond right away, he sighed again and leaned forward in his chair, resting his elbows on the table. "Enzo, I can see it in your eyes that something is eating at you, so you might as well tell me what it is."

I started to deny it, but he was right. Arguing with him was pointless. All it would do was piss him off and make things tense between us. However, I wasn't ready to tell him everything yet. Not until I was positive he would have my back when it came to Sera. So, I went for a partial truth. "You're right. There is something going on with me. And please forgive me, Luca, for imposing on our friendship like this, but I can't tell you what it is. At least not right now. Not yet."

"Does it have something to do with the girl we're looking for?"

I kept my mouth shut, unsurprised that he'd hit the nail right on the head. Luca wasn't the underboss for nothing, even if his father despised him. He had good instincts, and they usually led him right where he needed to be.

He tilted his head as he studied me, his gray eyes concerned. "Enzo, if you know where she is, you need to tell me. She's not worth starting a war over."

"I never said I knew where she is." I wasn't lying. At that very moment, I didn't know. I could guess she'd gone home after I dropped her off at the club. But since I wasn't with her, I couldn't know that for sure. I didn't even have a way to call her. Something that would need to be remedied immediately.

After a moment, he sighed and scratched his head. "Okay. We can play this your way for now. I just hope you know what you're doing."

I caught his gaze. "I would never put you or our family at risk, Luca." Ghosts danced around me as I made this vow. And for a moment, my heart ached with longing for the wife and son I'd lost so many years ago.

Reaching across the table, he put his hand over mine where it rested on the dark wood. "I know that, my friend. And that's the only reason I'm letting this go. For now," he added with a smile.

"Thank you," I told him sincerely. "I swear to you I will fill you in on everything as soon as I can."

He gave me a nod, and our conversation turned to business. A shop owner who was getting a little too full of himself and refused to pay his protection fee. And a new soldier who was having a hard time stomaching what he would have to do to change his mind. I promised Luca I would take care of things.

Shortly after, he made his way upstairs to join Veda, and I stayed where I was, enjoying the quiet. But before long, I was up and pacing the floor. I left my jacket and my sunglasses in the kitchen as I was alone in the house for the night. Then I made my way out to the main room where I took a right and headed toward Luca's office. I checked the interior, and continued down the hall.

I was restless, my skin tight and itchy. With Tristan gone, I would need to be here even more than usual. And that wouldn't give me much time to spend with Sera. I rubbed the back of my neck as I walked, trying to ease the tension there.

My mind flashed back to her sweet face, covered in my come. Seeing her marked by me like that should've calmed the beast inside of me. But instead, it only increased the urge to cover her with my scent, inside and out, so everyone would know she was mine.

I stopped walking. Jesus Christ. What the hell was I? A fucking animal?

Turning around, I went back the way I came until I stood at the top of the stairs that led down to the gym. I kept some extra workout clothes there, and right now, I really needed to hit something.

Tomorrow, I would have a phone sent to the club for Sera, with instructions that she was to keep it on her at all times. That would have to be enough until I could see her again.

CHAPTER 11

Serafina

In the light of the following day, the previous night seemed like a dream. Had I really agreed to be the sex toy of one of the scariest men in the mafia for money? A guy who'd ejaculated all over my face when I refused to give him a blow job?

Yes. Yes, I had.

Although I was nervous as all hell, I felt no lingering shame in the transaction I'd made. Last night had been the first sexual encounter I'd ever had with someone. But despite the innocence of my body, I was an educated woman, and there was nothing wrong with two consensual adults doing whatever the hell they wanted to together. Some might think living with Jade and working in this club had helped me come to that conclusion, but honestly, I'd always believed that. If people weren't hurting each other or anyone else, then who the hell cared what they're doing behind closed doors if it made them happy? Or who they're doing it with?

As I parked my car in the back lot at work, I was surprised to see security at the door. I was even more surprised when he walked right up to my car and scanned the area around us while he waited for me to get out.

"Is something going on?" I asked him.

"I'm to escort you inside, miss. And I'll be here to walk you to your car when you finish your shift."

He was big and brawny, even larger than Enzo. "Oh...uh...okay. Thank you." This was new, but I wasn't going to argue about extra safety measures with the hours I worked. It wasn't uncommon for homeless people, or worse, to be hanging outside the club when we left in the early morning hours.

He saw me safely inside and stepped in with me, taking up a position outside the break room where we had some tables and chairs, along with some snacks and drinks. I put the sandwich I'd brought in the fridge, then started taking off my coat as I went over to the wall of lockers. I found an empty one and stashed my phone, purse, and coat inside.

When I unzipped one of the pockets of my purse to drop my keys in there, I caught a glimpse of Enzo's watch that

I'd taken off his nightstand last night. Quickly, I zipped it back up before someone came in. I'd brought it with me so I could return it to him, assuming he came by tonight. He'd never really said anything when he dropped me off at my car last night about when I would see him again. Just that it would be "soon."

Grabbing a clean apron from the hooks on the wall next to the lockers, I tied it around my waist and then went to the bar to grab a notepad and pen. Bell was bartending tonight, and I was glad. She was much more pleasant to work with than Rob, but unfortunately, she only worked part-time so I only got to see her once a week. Twice if I was lucky. "Hey," I greeted her.

"Hey, Sera!" Bell returned my greeting with a smile. "How've you been, hon?"

"Good," I told her automatically. Bell was in her late thirties, tall and lean, with long blond hair she usually wore in some kind of braid and deep brown eyes. She looked amazing in her uniform of black slacks, a white shirt with the sleeves rolled up, a black vest, and bow tie.

"Oh, I have something for you," she told me as I was about to go check the table of three that had just come in.

"For me?"

She handed me a padded envelope with my name written on the front. I opened it up, and inside was a piece of paper and a cellphone. "Why am I getting a phone?" I asked her.

Bell shrugged, then walked over to the other end of the bar to get the drink order from a gentleman who'd just sat down.

I pulled out the piece of paper. Six numbers were written on it. A lock code? I tried it on the phone and the screen came to life, showing me there was a text message from "E."

With an uneasy feeling in my chest, I opened the message.

> Keep this phone on you at all times. This is only to be used for conversations between you and I. If it rings, I expect you to answer it. If a text comes in, you have five minutes to respond. If you don't answer my call or don't respond to my text, I will assume the worst and come find you. Trust me when I say, unless you're in immediate danger, you don't want that to happen for many reasons.

> I know your shift tonight is from 8pm to 2am. I will expect a response letting me know you have the phone in your possession no later than 8:05pm.

I CHECKED THE TIME. It was 8:04pm. Quickly, I punched out a text.

> I have the phone, but I'm not supposed to have it on me while I work. I'll need to put it in my locker.

His response came right away.

> You have the manager's permission to keep this one on you. If anyone gives you any shit about it, just let me know. Remember what I said.

Unsure, I looked around the bar, and then slid the phone into the front pocket of my apron, wondering what the hell I'd gotten myself into.

Two hours into my shift, I felt the phone vibrate against the front of the hip. When I set my tray down on the bar and pulled it out, I saw there was a text from Enzo.

> What time is your break?

I glanced at the time.

In five minutes.

BECAUSE I WAS NEW, I had to take my break early in the night. But I was just grateful they gave me thirty minutes together and not two fifteen-minute breaks, which wouldn't leave me with much time to eat.

I waited for a response, but none came, so I put the phone back into my apron and took the drinks Bell had set on my tray over to table five. I was starving, and I had to pee like nobody's business, but I tried not to think about my bulging bladder as I checked on my other tables and told the waitress who'd be covering for me who might need what while I was on break.

At 10pm exactly, my phone buzzed. I had just set my tray down on the bar and was heading toward the private restroom marked for employees only in the back of the bar near the break room. I waited until my most urgent need was taken care of and my hands were washed before I pulled it out and read the message.

Go into a bathroom stall.

I FROWNED.

> Why? I'm hungry and I'd like to eat while I have a break.

> Just do it, Sera. Let me know when you get there.

I LOOKED around the restroom like I would find the answer written on the wall somewhere. When I didn't, I slowly walked back into the stall I'd just come out of. Maybe if I did as he asked, he'd leave me alone and I could get on with my night.

> I'm in the stall.

> Put one foot on the toilet seat and take a picture of what's covering your pussy. Then send it to me.

HE WANTS me to send him panty pics? That's why I have this phone?

I don't remember agreeing to this.
Besides, I'm at work.

Send me the picture, Sera. Or I'll come
down there and throw you onto a table
in front of the entire goddamn club and
take it myself.

I HESITATED. Surely, he wouldn't do that.

I'm waiting, Sera.

I STARED down at the phone. A whole lot of emotions
were running through me right now, including disbelief,
anger, and annoyance. But the heavy feeling I suddenly
had in my lower belly overrode them all. Biting my lip, I
balanced my foot in its high-heeled shoe on the toilet,
stuck the phone underneath my skirt, and snapped a
picture of my ruffled panties. I had to take two more
before I got one that didn't look like a blurry, black glob of
nothing. Quickly, before I could change my mind, my
heart pounding beneath my ribcage, I sent it to him. His
response came right away.

Thank you.

I STAYED in the stall for five more minutes, waiting for my phone to go off again with another message, but it never did. Feeling slightly confused, and weirdly, more than a little turned on, I put the phone back into my apron and went to get my sandwich out of the fridge. It tasted like cardboard, but I swallowed it down, knowing I'd need the energy to get through the last six hours of my shift.

The rest of the night went by without interruption from the phone in my pocket, and when I finally closed out for the night and said goodnight to the rest of the staff, I limped out to my car with the security guard beside me. My feet were fucking killing me. He didn't try to assist me, but instead kept scanning the lot like he expected monsters to jump out from behind the parked cars at any moment.

And even though I told myself I wouldn't do it, I couldn't help but look for a blacked-out SUV waiting for me in the lot. But it wasn't there. Just my car and Bell's, and what I would guess was the security guard's.

I pulled out the phone and checked it, but there were no messages I might have missed as I got into the car. I thought about messaging him to tell him I had his watch, but just the thought made my cheeks heat with embarrassment. Plus, it was late. He was probably sleeping. So, I laid the phone down on the passenger seat next to my purse and started the car. The security guard raised his hand in a wave as I drove away, and I watched him in my rearview mirror as he walked over to the car I didn't recognize. Wasn't he going to wait for Bell? Should I stop and tell him she was still in there?

But before I could make up my mind, he was pulling away.

I headed back to Jade's, feeling weirdly disconcerted, a lot nervous, and if I were going to be honest with myself, a little let down. It took me a while to fall asleep that night, but once I did, I slept like the dead, waking up just in time to make some dinner and get ready for my next shift. Either Jade had stayed out all night, which wasn't unusual, or she'd snuck in while I was asleep and was still crashed out in her bedroom. Eating and getting ready had managed to keep me distracted for a while. But now my anxiety was back in full force as I thought of something.

Was he expecting me to just show up at his hotel every night? Or was I supposed to just go about my business and wait for him to contact me? He hadn't said anything, and since I'd never done anything like this before, I wasn't sure what he expected of me.

I checked my phone again. Nothing. So I went into work and tried to forget about the fact that I hadn't heard from him all day. When my shift was done, I counted out my tips and decided to just go home. But by the time I got back to Jade's apartment, I was a frazzled mess. Part of me was hoping he'd found out where she lived somehow and would be here waiting for me, and the other part was trying to convince myself I needed to pack a bag and run away as fast as I could before he found me again.

My phone vibrated and made a little ding sound right after I made it through the door and set my stuff down on the counter. My heart began to pound as I picked up the phone and opened the text message.

Goodnight, baby girl.

I paused for a moment, and then typed,

Goodnight.

I turned off the screen and set the phone back down on the counter. Then, keeping my mind carefully blank, I went in and took a shower and pulled on a nightshirt and some pajama shorts. I went to the fridge, but we were out of yogurt, so I added it to my grocery list and grabbed a banana instead, taking it and a glass of water with me over to the couch. Setting them on the coffee table, I unfolded the blanket lying at the foot, spread it over the couch cushions, then picked up the remote and turned on Netflix.

I was halfway through the next episode of the show I was watching when the phone on the counter rang. Throwing the blanket off my lap, I jumped up off the couch and ran over to answer it. "Hello?"

"What are you wearing, Sera?"

His voice made shivers skate over my skin. I walked back over to the couch and turned down the volume on the television. "Seriously?" I asked him.

"I want to know what you sleep in," was his response.

Looking down at myself because I'd completely forgotten if I was even wearing clothes the moment I heard his voice, I told him, "A dark blue nightshirt and a pair of red plaid pajama shorts. Probably not the sexy vision you were hoping for."

But he just said, "That's exactly the vision I was hoping for. Goodnight, baby girl."

"Wait," I said before he could hang up. "Are you still there?"

"Yes."

"Um. I was just wondering when I can expect to see you again. I've never done this type of thing before and I...I wasn't sure if..." I trailed off.

I heard him inhale and exhale, like he was sighing. "I'm not sure," he told me, and I could hear the frustration in his tone. "But when you do, I'd like my watch back."

I started to tell him I'd grabbed it by mistake, but he interrupted me before I could give him the lame excuse I always gave everyone when I actually had to hand something back to them.

"Why do you do that?"

"Do what?" I asked, even though I knew exactly what he was talking about.

"Steal things," he said. "I know you don't do it for money. Is it just for fun?"

My eyes stung with tears, and I blinked them back, although I could still hear them in my voice. "No."

"Then tell me why."

"I don't know why," I whispered.

He was quiet for a few seconds. "Okay. Get some sleep, Sera."

Then he hung up the phone.

"Okay," I said softly. Setting the phone on the table, I went back to my purse and grabbed the charging cord that had come with it, plugging it in. Then I grabbed Enzo's watch and put it on my arm. It was too big for my wrist, so I slid it up to just beneath my elbow. Leaving it there, I went back over to the couch and hit play on the remote.

I didn't sleep much that night.

Or the next.

CHAPTER 12

Enzo

The screaming.

I'd never forget the sound of it. Or how helpless I'd felt. How after a while my wife's voice was so raw, she barely made any sound at all, even though her mouth was wide open and I was afraid she would permanently damage her vocal cords. Yet still, she screamed. Her eyes bulging with horror. Her body shaking with the force of it.

Alessandra's screams still haunted my dreams.

I lurched up and off the couch where I must've fallen asleep, a sick feeling in my stomach and my wife's shock and heartbreak still fresh in my ears. Sweat dripped down my face and spine, soaking through my white dress shirt and making it stick to my back. My eyes were wild as they shot around Luca's office until gradually my heart slowed and my breaths became less labored.

A dream. It was only a fucking dream. I'd fallen asleep on the couch in Luca's office.

Checking my phone, I saw it was 3:17am. I tossed it down on the couch and went over to pour myself a whiskey. It wouldn't help keep me awake, but that was okay. There were so many alarms set on this house a cat couldn't walk across the yard without me knowing about it. And maybe it would help ward off the nightmares. My wife was dead now, as was the son we'd had together, yet recently, they wouldn't stop haunting me.

For good reason.

They'd died fifteen years ago, when I was a very young man. I couldn't save them. They'd left me all alone, as my parents had before them. And if it hadn't been for Luca and Tristan, I would've followed them from this world. But eventually, the pain and loneliness became bearable, if not forgotten. The paralyzing terror that it would happen again, however, that shit was still very much alive.

Taking my glass with me, I walked around the house, double checking the security system and checking in with the soldiers outside. All was quiet as Luca and Veda slept.

By the time I made it back to the office for a refill, the screams that had woken me were nothing more than a vague memory I'd stuffed back down into the compartment of my brain I reserved for them. The one I never, ever, opened when I was awake and conscious. They only pushed their way out when I was asleep. It had happened often right after the funerals, but I hadn't dreamed of them now for a long time. And I knew it was Sera that was bringing them back. And the way I felt about her.

I turned my mind to what had been discussed at tonight's meeting with Luca and Gino to distract myself. Yet my skin still felt too tight. My mouth dry, despite the whiskey I was chugging like water. I was too fucking restless. I needed something more. Something to take the edge off.

Grabbing my phone off the couch, I opened the screen and tapped in the number I knew from memory. For both of our safety, I didn't have it in my contacts. After a few rings, she answered, her voice soft with sleep.

"Hello?"

"Where are you?"

There was a pause on the other end of the line. "Home."

"Tell me what you're wearing."

This time, she didn't hesitate. "Dark gray sleep shorts and an old concert T-shirt I found at Goodwill." She yawned into the phone.

"What band?"

"Guns and Roses."

"'The Appetite Tour?"

"I think so."

I knew exactly the shirt she was describing. "Are your clothes tight or loose?"

"Loose."

Good. Walking over to the door, I checked the hall, listening for anyone who might be up and around, then closed it and turned the lock. "Are you wearing anything underneath?"

She was beginning to sound a little more awake now. "No."

"Are your feet bare?"

"Yes."

"Hair up or down?"

"Down."

I sat on the couch with my knees spread wide and leaned back against the leather cushions, unbuttoning the top five buttons of my dress shirt. "Are you laying down?"

"Yes."

"On a bed?"

"A couch."

A cold feeling swept through me. "Do you always sleep on a couch?"

"Yes."

I didn't like the thought of her crashing on somebody's couch. She deserved to be in a bed with an expensive mattress, fancy sheets, and a soft comforter with pillows piled around her. But right now, I had other things on my mind, so I put that away for later. "Blanket?"

"Yes."

"Good, keep it on you." I closed my eyes, imagining her just as she said. The picture was near perfect. "I want to make you come, Sera. Will you let me do that?"

There was a sharp intake of breath. "Um. I don't think that's a good idea. Jade is here. She's in her room, and I don't know if she's still awake."

So, she was living with Jade. "Then you'll just have to be quiet."

"And if I don't want to do this?"

"Then I'll consider our agreement null and void, and your father's goons will be on their way to fetch you within fifteen minutes. Your choice, Sera." I gave her a few moments to decide.

I heard her heavy sigh, and then she said in a resigned voice, "What do you want me to do?"

"Lay the phone on the pillow by your ear."

"Okay."

"Can you still hear me?"

"Yes."

"Are both of your hands free?"

"Yes." Her voice was barely more than a whisper.

"With your right hand, find the hem of your shirt and slip it underneath. Then slowly...slowly...slide it up over your stomach until you find your breast. And Sera?"

"Yes?"

"I'll know if you're faking. So don't fucking lie to me about what you're doing or feeling. Understood?"

After a moment, she said, "Understood."

"Is your hand on your breast?"

"Yes."

"Close your eyes and tell me, what does it feel like?"

"What?"

"What does it feel like? Soft? Hard? Does it fill your palm?"

"Um, soft. And...uh..." She cleared her throat. "It's too big to fit in my palm."

So, she wasn't wearing any kind of push up when she wore that pink dress. I wanted to ask her to give me a detailed description of her breast, including the areola and nipple. Or, better yet, to send me a picture. With her pink hair and pale skin, it seemed obvious they would be a light pink. However, Sera was Italian. So I would bet money they were a darker mauve. My mouth watered at the thought.

"Is your nipple hard?"

"Yes."

"Pinch it between your thumb and forefinger and tell me what you feel. Not too hard," I told her. "Not yet." I heard her intake of breath. "What do you feel?"

"Pain."

"And what else?"

"Um...it made my stomach tighten. Low in my stomach."

I shifted on the couch and adjusted myself in my pants. "Take both of your breasts in your hands and squeeze them, then roll your nipples between your fingers."

"Okay." Her voice was quiet and a bit breathless.

I scrubbed my hand over my face. "Tell me what you're doing," I ordered in a hard voice.

She cleared her throat, and in my mind, I could see the blood coloring her face and chest. "I'm...um..."

I heard her hesitation to voice the words out loud. "Sera, don't be shy with me, baby girl. Just thinking of you like this has me so fucking turned on. Tell me, so I can see you."

"I'm...I'm lifting my breasts in my hands and squeezing, then letting them go and rubbing the center of my palms over my nipples."

"Thank you. How does that feel?"

"It feels good."

It will feel so much fucking better when I'm doing it. "Keep doing what you're doing, but now imagine it's my hands touching you. Wet your thumb and rub it over your nipple and imagine it's my tongue." I listened to her breathing change. Every breath coming closer together, faster and shorter. "Am I there with you, baby girl? Can you feel me?"

"Yes," she said breathlessly.

"Is your heart pounding? Are you getting wet for me? I want you soaking wet, Sera."

Her moan was my answer.

With one hand, I opened my shirt the rest of the way so it fell to the sides, then unfastened my pants and shoved down the front of my boxer briefs until my cock was free. I was already fucking hard, the tip dripping with pre-come. I'd wanted to make this last, but she was so fucking responsive, I didn't think it was going to be possible this time.

Throwing my head back against the couch cushion, I fisted myself in my free hand. "I'm so fucking hard for you, Sera. I'm about to come imagining you touching yourself. Do you want to come with me?"

"Yes," she whispered.

"Do you still have the blanket covering you?"

"Yes."

"Take off your shorts," I told her. "Tell me when they're off."

I heard her rustling around. "Okay," she said after a few seconds. "They're off."

"Good girl. Slide one foot up and bend your knee. Leave the other leg down. Now put your left hand back under your shirt and squeeze your breast again. With your right hand, slide your middle finger between the folds of your pussy."

There was a sharp intake of breath. *Ahh...fuck me.* I gripped my cock near the base in an effort to keep myself in check. "Are you wet, Sera?"

"Yes."

"Are you wet enough to spread it up to your clit?"

"Yes."

"Do that," I ordered. "Do you want to add another finger?"

Her breath caught. "Yes."

"Okay, baby. Go ahead. Do you feel how wet you are?"

"Yes."

"Run your fingers through your pussy for me, Sera. Spread it all over, then come back up to your clit." I knew when she was there by the sweet sounds she made. I didn't even have to ask. "Touch yourself the way you like. Is your other hand still on your breast?" My voice was low and rough.

"Yes."

"When you feel the first wave of your orgasm, I want you to pinch your nipple hard. Do you understand?"

"That will hurt."

"Yes," I told her. "It will. But it will be worth it, baby. Just trust me."

For a few seconds, I just listened to her breathing as I fisted my cock, rubbing it up and squeezing the head, then back down to the base. "Go a little bit faster now. Are you ready for that?"

"Yes." Her voice was needy. "Oh, god."

I jerked myself off faster. "That's it, baby. I want to hear you come for me."

"Enzo..."

My name left her lips on a sweet, whispery moan, and I wanted to jump through the goddamn phone. "I'm here,

Sera. Come on, baby. Come for me. I want to hear you come for me because I'm about to fucking bust out of my skin here."

"I'm so close."

This time I heard frustration. "I want to touch you, Sera. So fucking bad. I want to taste the skin on your throat, and suck your nipples into my mouth so I can roll them between my teeth. Then I want to kiss every fucking inch of your body. I want to taste your sweet pussy until you feel so good, I have to hold you down. And then I want you to come in my mouth, baby. I want to taste you. Fuck, Sera."

I heard her whimper quietly, and I could tell she was trying to keep quiet.

"Sera."

She made a small noise.

"Come for me, baby." I ordered, my own orgasm powering down my spine. "Come for me NOW."

As soon as I heard her breath catch, I let myself loose. "Fuck. Fuck!" Hot spurts of come landed on my stomach, over and over as I moaned her name.

After, I sat there with my hand on my softening cock and listened to her breathing.

"Enzo?"

"Yeah, baby?"

There was a long pause, and then she said quietly, "I wish you were here." And then she hung up the phone.

Next time, I will be, Sera.

Tossing the phone back onto the couch, I got up and went into Luca's bathroom to clean myself up. I thought about getting on the computer and finding out where Jade's place was. But then I reined myself in. Jade respected my privacy, the least I could do was respect hers. Besides, I was on duty. Knowing where she was would just make it that much fucking harder to keep my ass here, where it belonged.

Throwing some water on my face, I washed my hands and grabbed the small towel off the rack to dry off my face and stomach. My hands had stopped shaking, and I felt calmer, if not completely back to normal.

When I was finished in the bathroom, I went over and unlocked the door and did another check through the house. As I walked, I thought about what I was doing, trying to figure out why I was risking my life for this woman. What it was about her that made me unable to leave her alone. But I couldn't give it a name. All I knew was that from the moment she showed up at my door in that tacky pink bandage dress, I'd felt a rush of possession like nothing I'd ever felt before. Sera was mine. And this time, no one was going to take her away from me.

I just had to figure out a way to keep her without making her hate me.

CHAPTER 13

Serafina

I went into work with my face flaming and my heart beating a staccato rhythm in my chest, half excited and half terrified that Enzo would be there. I was embarrassed by my behavior on the phone the night before. I'd been sound asleep when Enzo had called, dreaming of something I couldn't remember the moment I answered the phone and heard his voice. He'd sounded different somehow. Still as bossy as usual, but also like he...needed me. There'd been something raw and desperate in his voice, and I couldn't help but respond to it.

So I did as he told me and closed my eyes, imagining it was Enzo's hands touching me and not my own...I'd never come so fast in my life. But it wasn't the phone sex I was embarrassed about. It was what I'd said when it was over about how I wished he'd been there. It was stupid of me to say it out loud. I shouldn't have opened myself up that way. That being said, I thought for sure he would make an appearance tonight.

But he wasn't at the club when I arrived. Nor was he there when I got off of break. I took a deep breath for the first time all night and felt some of the tension leave my shoulders. I was way too nervous about seeing him again. That phone call last night...it was different from the night he'd shoved his cock in my face. And I wasn't talking about consent. Even over the phone, the intimacy was strange to me. It left me with an unfamiliar feeling of connection to another person for the first time in my life. But at the same time, I felt way too vulnerable. And saying things that, although truly felt at the time, I never should've voiced out loud.

"Hey, sweetheart! Can I get another drink?"

I glanced up from the table I was clearing to see a man who was sitting with a friend, holding up an empty glass. He wasn't in my section, but I went over to see what he needed anyway. Customers got what they wanted around here, and if he wanted me to get him another drink, that's what I had to do until his server reappeared.

Balancing the dirty dishes and napkins on my tray, I went over to his table with a smile on my face. "Of course!" I told him brightly. "What are you drinking?"

Eyes on my cleavage, he said, "Scotch. Neat. And make sure it's top shelf. Not the cheap crap."

My smile never wavered. "Absolutely." Turning my attention to his friend, I asked, "What about you? Would you like anything?"

He shook his head, his eyes never leaving one of the women sitting at the bar. "I'm good. Thanks."

"Alright, I'll be right back with your scotch," I told the first man.

"Hey, wait a minute."

I shifted the heavy tray so most of the weight was on my other hand. My arms were beginning to ache. "Did you change your mind?"

He shook his head, and I felt the back of his fingers brush the bare skin on my leg right above the stocking. "No. But I think I'd like to add to my order."

I shifted away from him, but kept my smile firmly in place. "Sure. What else would you like?"

"You. Sitting on my cock for the rest of the night."

I wasn't shocked by his request. I'd known immediately by the way he was looking at me that this one would be a handful. "Sorry, I'm not on the menu," I told him. "I'm just a server. However, there are quite a few lovely ladies over by the bar who I'm sure would love to be your date tonight."

His expression grew hard. "I don't want them. I want you." Fast as a snake, his hand shot out and went up under my skirt. He wrapped it around the inside of my thigh, brushing against my panties, his fingers digging hard into my flesh.

This wasn't the first time I'd been in this situation, but it was definitely the first time anyone had grabbed me by the leg. Smart of him, though, being that I had a heavy tray in my hands with empty glasses piled on it. "Sir, you need to remove your hand. I'm sorry, but I'm not for sale. My job is to serve you drinks. That's it. However, if you'd like me to, I will happily introduce you to one of the ladies here who are not waiting on tables."

The entire time I was talking, his hand had been caressing the inside of my thigh. And now his thumb began to wander, pressing against my perineum over my ruffled panties as he searched for an entrance to my body. I jumped and tried to pull away, but he only gripped my thigh tighter. I felt his nails digging into my skin. "Let me go," I said loudly in a firm voice. Glancing around, I looked for the new security guard, but he was nowhere to be found.

"Tell me what time you get off, little girl, and I'll let you get back to your tables."

I tried to catch the attention of the other man to see if he would help me before I was forced to make a scene, but he was ignoring us completely, his eyes on a redhead in a black sequined dress.

Alright then, scene it was.

I was just lifting my full tray to send it crashing into his lap when it was grabbed out of my hands. Startled, I swung my head around to find the new security guy beside me.

He set the tray down on the table, then very purposefully looked at the man whose hand was still up my dress and pushed his jacket back from his hip, revealing the pistol on his hip. "Remove your hand from the lady," he ordered. "Now."

Although he never raised his voice, his meaning was clear. The man at the table smirked, his eyes going from the security guard to the gun. After a moment, he let go of my leg as quickly as he'd grabbed it. As soon as he released me, I took a few steps back, placing myself well out of his reach.

The man at the table put both hands in the air and smiled. "Hey now, no need for all this. I was just trying to ask for a date, is all."

"Sera is not for sale," the guard told him. "Nor is she available for a 'date' of any kind. I strongly suggest you look elsewhere." He picked up my tray and handed it to me.

"Thank you," I told him.

He gave me a nod and held out his arm, indicating for me to go before him. With one last warning look for the man at the table, he escorted me over to the bar. "I apologize, I didn't see what was happening sooner. I was in the restroom."

"Oh, that's okay," I assured him. "You can't watch everyone all the time."

The guard frowned. "I think you misunderstand. I'm only here to watch over you, miss."

I'd been going through my tickets, but when he said that, I froze and looked up at him. "What?"

"I'm here for you," he repeated. "To protect you. Did Mr. Delligatti not tell you?"

"No," I told him. "He didn't."

A smile teased the corner of his mouth, and I realized that he wasn't a bad looking guy. He actually reminded me a little of a larger version of Jason Statham. "Well, now you know. And again, I apologize for not being there sooner."

I just nodded, not sure how to feel about what he'd just told me.

The rest of the night went by quickly and without incident. I made decent tips, and the man with the hands didn't so much as look my way the rest of the night. Jade was still out when I got home, so I grabbed my nightclothes and went into her bathroom to take a shower. My thigh hurt where that guy had grabbed me, so I put one foot up on the counter and tried to see the damage in the mirror over the sink. There was a hand-sized red print on my skin, a little darker where his fingertips dug into me with a couple of crescent-shaped cuts from his nails. I cursed him and all men as I saw the marks he'd left on me. That was probably going to leave a few bruises.

I washed my leg really well in the shower and put some antibiotic ointment on the small cuts when I got out. God knows what could've been under his nails.

Exhausted, I crawled into the bed I'd made on the couch, leaving the phone Enzo had given me on the coffee table. A minute later, I rolled over, picked it up, and turned it off. He could do without me for one night. Besides, last night was the first time he'd called me in the middle of the night like that. What were the chances that he'd do it again?

When I woke up, there was a message on my phone.

I want to see you touch yourself.

FOLLOWED BY:

Sera?

M*y body came instantly awake even* as I frowned in confusion. Was he just letting me know, or was he requesting a video or something?

> I'm here. I was sleeping.

H*e'd sent* the message a few hours before. While I waited for him to respond, I snuck into Jade's bathroom to pee and brush my teeth, since I'd left my toothbrush in there the night before, leaving the phone on the coffee table so it didn't go off and wake her. She was snoring lightly, lying on her back with a black satin eye cover over her eyes and one boob precariously close to falling out of the black silk nightgown she was wearing. Closing the bedroom door behind me, I tiptoed to the kitchen to get some coffee, grabbing the phone again as I passed. I'd have to wake her up in an hour so we could get something to eat and get ready for work. It buzzed in my hand.

> Did you not hear the phone?

I *almost told him*, no, I'd shut the damn thing off. But I didn't think he'd appreciate that comment. However, I refused to apologize for sleeping. So I just said,

No, I didn't. I was exhausted.

THERE WAS A LONG PAUSE. Then,

I still want to see you touch yourself.

STILL FEELING that little kick of rebellion, I answered,

I guess you'll just have to wait until I see you again.

FEELING QUITE PROUD OF MYSELF, I left the phone on the counter and started making some coffee. When it pinged with a new text message, I didn't run over there right away, but waited until I had my drink in my hands.

I'll see you tonight. Pack a change of clothes.

SEE ME. Not call me. Not text me. My eyes went wide. Shit. That didn't go the way I thought it would.

> Tonight? I have to work.

> I know.

HE PROBABLY DID. It wouldn't surprise me if he received a copy of my schedule every week.

> What if I have plans?

IT TOOK a minute to get his reply.

> Change them. I have to go. I'll see you tonight, Sera. Don't forget to pack a bag.

JUST LIKE THAT. I took a deep breath, bracing myself for the night to come. It was time for me to hold up my end of our bargain up close and personal. My stomach tightened with nerves and, I had to admit, excitement. But surprisingly, no fear.

After tonight, I would no longer be a virgin.

CHAPTER 14

Enzo

It's been a week since I've seen Sera, and I was about to jump out of my skin. I knew Luca would've given me some time off if I'd asked him, but I couldn't say anything to him without giving her away, so I gritted my teeth and carried out my duties. This was a critical time for us. It was common knowledge now that Luca was planning to make a play for his father's position of Boss, and that made him vulnerable to those who were happy with things the way they were, or who were gunning for the position themselves.

However, I couldn't leave her alone entirely. I tried. I tried to push her out of my head. But I ached to see her face. To hear her voice. And I craved other things. Things I had no business needing from her. *Especially* not from her.

But there was no denying it. I wanted Sera to the point that it made me fucking crazy, and yet I couldn't have her. Not yet. And that made her dangerous both to me and to those I was protecting.

I hurried through my last drop off of product for Luca and left my partner for the day back off at the house. By the time I walked into the club where Sera worked, my blood was practically vibrating with the need to get her alone where I could talk to her, touch her. Feel the way she trembled. I craved the little sounds she'd made on the phone, the ones that played on repeat in my head. I wanted to hear them in person. Right in my fucking ear as I made her come over and over again.

And tonight, I finally had a night off.

When I walked in, the bartender—a woman—recognized me right away and pointed to one of the empty tables in Sera's section. It was good to know the owner had spread the word about our arrangement.

I spotted her immediately. She was taking an order from a table of three men, all around my age or older. As I watched her, I realized there was something off with the way she was standing. It took me a moment before I finally realized what it was. She was shielding herself behind the empty chair, just out of touching range from the man on her right. This wasn't the usual routine for the waitstaff. Normally, she would stand way too fucking close to whoever she thought would give her the biggest tip, sucking on that damn lollipop that was always in her mouth. I knew this because it made me fucking crazy to see her that close to another man. Bending over their table every chance she got to give them a good look at her cleavage. Only copious amounts of whiskey had kept me in my chair the last time I was here.

But not tonight. Tonight she appeared skittish, and it was more than fucking obvious that one guy, at least—some *stronzo* who was obviously trying, and failing, to look like the older brother in that television show, Supernatural— was completely enamored with her in that little baby doll dress and fuck me heels.

I continued to watch her, wondering if I was imagining things. Perhaps there was a spill on the floor or some other reason she was standing so far away from the table. Something I couldn't see.

Once she had their order, she smiled and headed over to the bar, stopping to leave a check with one of her other tables. She didn't appear distraught in any way, so I figured that perhaps I was wrong and I was making too much out of nothing. However, I made a living by noticing little nuances other people missed, and I couldn't get rid of the nagging feeling that something wasn't right.

Sera spotted me while she stood at the bar waiting for her drink order. Her smoky eyes went wide, and she froze with her pen hovering in the air above her order pad. I fought a smile when I saw her lift her chin, like she was preparing herself for battle. She said something to the bartender as she tucked her pen and pad back into her black silk apron and then headed toward me.

My eyes soaked in her appearance, and I wanted more than anything to take off these damn sunglasses so I could see all of the colors of Sera without anything dimming them. Her pink hair, bright eyes, translucent skin. Colors that should contrast and yet were completely perfect together.

When she got to my table, she stood awkwardly for a few seconds before saying, "You're here," in a tone that was less than enthusiastic.

I felt my smile tugging at the corners of my lips at her surprise. "I am. Would you get me a whiskey, please? Neat."

"Oh, um. Of course. Anything else? Water? A snack from the kitchen?"

"Just whiskey."

She wrote it down and left to put in my drink order.

While I waited for my drink, I pulled out my phone to check in with Tristan, who was still at Gino's. "Everything good?"

"Not yet," he told me. "But it will be. Two of our soldiers are missing." He paused. "Where are you?"

"Just getting a drink. I need to decompress."

"Who's covering Luca?"

I filled him in on everything that was going on back at the lake house so he wouldn't worry. Sera came over with my drink while I was talking, and I grabbed her arm so she wouldn't walk away before I got off the phone.

She flinched when I touched her. It wasn't a big movement, and if I hadn't been paying attention, I wouldn't have noticed it at all. I frowned, staring up at her face as she tried to smile to cover her reaction. Slowly, I turned her arm over so the inside was facing up and moved my hand down to her wrist. Her skin wasn't marred in any way. But that did nothing to throw off my suspicions. "T, I need to go. I'll call you later." Making sure the call was disconnected, I put my phone back inside my jacket. "Why are you flinching when I touch you?"

She opened her mouth, and I could see she was about to deny it happened. But then her eyes searched for mine behind my glasses and her expression changed. "You just took me by surprise. I have to be on guard when I'm here, you know? It was just an automatic reaction."

I caressed the inside of her wrist with my thumb, feeling her pulse flutter nervously. "Do your customers often get out of line?"

She shook her head. "Just once in a while."

My blood grew hot. "If I ever see anyone lay a hand on you, I'll kill them."

She stared down at me for a long time. "I believe you," she said, so quietly I almost didn't hear her. Then she blinked a few times fast and gently pulled her arm from my grip. "I need to check my other tables."

Picking up my whiskey, I took a sip. But my eyes never left her perfect face. "I'll be here."

Her eyes traveled over my face, and again, I sensed that she was nervous. Then she turned and went over to the table she was serving when I arrived. Her step faltered when she got close, and she quickly sidestepped to avoid the touch of the man to the right who reached out like he was going to rest his hand on her hip. The one she seemed to be avoiding earlier.

My attention zeroed in on him. He was mouthing off to her, and he didn't look happy that she was avoiding him. When he tried to grab her again as she collected the empty glasses from the table, she jumped back out of his reach, nearly upsetting the tray in her hands. Once more she said something to him, then the others, then she headed to the bar, shooting me a look from the corner of her eye and quickly turning away when she saw that I was watching.

Noticing the look she'd given me, the guy who was giving her a hard time shot a heated glance my way. I held his stare as I called over one of the other waitresses. The dark-haired one in the harem costume. "Who is that man?" I asked her.

"I'm not sure," she told me. "But I can find out for you."

I pulled out my wallet and handed her a hundred-dollar bill. "Do that for me, please. And do not let Sera overhear you."

She took the money and headed to the bar where Sera was still waiting for her drink orders. Once Sera was gone, I watched as she got the bartender's attention and subtly pointed at the guy at the other table and then nodded in my direction. A minute later, she passed by my table. "His name is Derek Jonak. He owns a few local companies and thinks he's a big deal. That's all I could find out."

"Thank you," I told her. She gave me a nod and walked away to greet a customer who'd just come in.

It took me a total of five minutes to find out his age, marital status, every company the guy owned, what he was worth, who his parents were, how many siblings he had, where he grew up, his phone number, and his home address. I saved the information for future use should the need arise. Right now, he was just being annoying. And as much as I would like to go over there and break every bone in his hands, I didn't think it would earn me any favor in Sera's eyes. And I found I didn't like the thought of her looking at me as if I were a monster. However, if he continued with his behavior, further action may need to be taken.

I made some more phone calls while I watched Sera move around the room, stepping outside when needed to disguise my location. This club was under Luca's protection, but it wasn't a place anyone in *La Cosa Nostra* frequented. Most of us stuck to Gino's restaurant and Luca's club out of loyalty. I was one of the few who chose to keep company with professional women of Jade's caliber.

Sera was standing just inside the door waiting for me as I finished up my last call. She had her coat on and her bag over her arm. "I'm on break," she explained when I came in.

I inhaled, taking in her scent of coconuts and tropical flowers. "Are you hungry?"

"Yes."

The way she said it brought back flashes of her saying the same thing as I ordered her to touch herself over the phone. My body tightened. "Come on. We'll get you something to eat."

"Oh, um..." She pointed over her shoulder back into the club. "I actually brought a sandwich. I don't have time for much else."

I frowned. "They expect you to work all night on a sandwich?"

She smiled at me. It wasn't a full-on smile, but it made something funny happen in my gut. "I don't think they care about what we eat. Or if we eat at all, to be honest. As long as I'm back on the floor when I'm supposed to be, and I make the customers happy and don't spill any drinks."

I stared at her. I couldn't believe what I was hearing, although it shouldn't surprise me. Pulling my cell phone out of my pocket, I called the owner whose name I still couldn't remember. "It's me," I told him when he answered. "I'm taking Sera to get something to eat, and she will be late getting back. And she will need a longer break from now on. An hour minimum. If she wants to come back before that, fine. But she will have an hour." Taking the phone away from my ear, I tapped the screen and ended the call. "Let's go," I told her as I put it back into my inside pocket. "We don't have much time."

"What the hell did you just do?"

I cocked my head. "You need to have enough time to eat, Sera. Hell, just getting back and forth to a restaurant anywhere near here will take nearly half your break. That's ridiculous."

She was still staring at me with her mouth hanging open, the soft lighting of the club behind her haloing her pink pigtails. "Enzo, you can't just walk in here and order the people who run this place to give me special treatment."

"Yes, I can. And I just did. Now come on. I know you have to be hungry, and you're wasting your break standing here arguing with me." I held out my hand.

After a moment, she took it, and I drew a calming breath once I felt her fingers wrapped within mine.

But she wasn't done with me yet. "Enzo, you can't demand that I have special treatment just because of our...agreement."

"Yes, I can."

"No, you can't! It's bad enough you come in here and sit at that table all night watching me like some kind of stalker. I need to work. I want to work. And I don't want to be treated any differently than anyone else. I like my co-workers, for the most part—"

I glanced over at her as we reached the SUV, but she didn't go into further detail.

"—and if you keep doing shit like this, everyone will hate me. I like this job. It's the first time in my life I've ever been able to support myself. To make my own money. To be at all independent. And I can only do it because of the level of discretion here. If everyone has it in for me because they think I'm some kind of mafia princess, I'll end up getting fired, and I'll have to leave town with the little bit I've saved up, which isn't nearly enough to get me out of my father's reach."

She stopped to take a breath. By this time, she was in the passenger seat, and I was waiting for her to finish before I closed her door. "I won't allow them to fire you, Sera."

Closing her eyes, her chin fell to her chest, and she rubbed her forehead with her fingertips. "Did you not hear anything I just said? That's not the point." Lifting her head, she gave me an entreating look.

"I heard you," I told her. "I just don't want you to worry about something that isn't going to happen. Now let's go eat. I'm hungry."

After I was in the car and we were pulling out of the lot, she said, "I'm not taking more than my thirty minutes after tonight."

I glanced over at her and sighed. "Then I'll have food delivered for you while you're here."

"You don't have to do that."

"I know."

"I'm fine with a sandwich, really. I eat when I get home."

"Stop arguing with me, Sera."

I felt her eyes on me a moment longer, and then she turned to look out the windshield. "I can't go into a restaurant dressed like this."

Reaching over, I covered her hand with mine. "Stop worrying. It's fine." The place I was taking her had a private room, and her coat would cover her until we got in there.

She was quiet until I pulled up to the restaurant a few minutes later. "I hope you like Asian food," I told her. "I'm sorry, I should've asked."

"I love Asian food." She smiled at me again, bigger this time, and my heart stuttered in my chest. If we got through this meal without me tearing off those ruffled panties she wore and fucking her against the wall, it would be a goddamned miracle.

I helped her out of the car and made sure she was sufficiently covered before escorting her inside. The manager herself greeted us at the door. "Mr. Enzo!"

"Hi, Lynn. Is the back room available?"

"Of course!" Gathering some menus, she led us through the restaurant to the backroom. I ate here often, although usually I was by myself, and I asked for the back room because it made me nervous to eat in the dining room. Nearly the entire front wall was made of windows, putting anyone who dined there on full display, and the last thing I wanted was for someone who had it out for me or Luca to shoot up the place because I was stupid enough to show them I was there.

"This place is so nice," Sera told me once we were seated at the single table. It was large, meant to seat up to sixteen people, and took up most of the space. As the focal point of the room, it was also a work of art, a rich cherry wood, the center carved with scenes from Chinese folklore. We sat at the end furthest from the door, with my back to the wall and Sera seated to my right. The walls were covered with black and gold wallpaper, and gold wall sconces lit the room with soft, warm light.

In this lighting, Sera's skin appeared nearly translucent, her eyes, lips, and hair darker than they actually were, and I couldn't stop looking at her. I'd helped her take off her coat and laid it over the back of her chair, and now my eyes traveled over her face, her throat, the elegant curve of her collarbones, and down to the curves of flesh that pushed up from the neckline of her dress. She was stunning in this light. And completely seductive.

I started to reach for her when there was a knock at the door and the server came in. Pulling my hand back, I looked down at my menu. She gave us a small bow and asked if we were ready to order.

"Get whatever you'd like," I told Sera.

She smiled at the girl and ordered a chicken dish and some iced tea. I put in my own order that included a full-bodied Malbec wine and handed the server our menus. Once we were alone again, I watched Sera as she nervously clenched her hands together in her lap. She looked around the room, down the long table, anywhere but at me.

"Why are you so nervous? Are you having second thoughts?" Not that it would matter. Not to me. This beguiling woman wasn't going anywhere until I had the chance to fuck her as many times as I wanted. I'd lost control the other night. I hadn't meant to. It had taken the edge off, but I was nowhere near satiated. Like eating a few nuts when you were starving.

She didn't try to play it off or pretend that she didn't know what I was talking about. "No," she told me. "I just don't know what to do with myself when you stare at me like that."

"Like what?"

Her eyes searched mine. "Like you're going to pounce on me without warning."

The door opened, and the server came in with our drinks and a dish with two spring rolls and a dipping sauce. Other than a cursory glance and a nod of thanks, I didn't take my eyes from Sera. I couldn't. I was bedazzled, even as she sat there in that ridiculous outfit with her hair in pigtails, meant to look like a little girl. But she did not look like a girl to me. She was a woman. And I couldn't wait to be inside of her. "Did you bring a change of clothes like I told you?"

She'd been watching the server leave, but at this, she turned her face back to me. Her eyes met mine and then fell to her drink. She wrapped her hand around the glass. "Yes," she said softly, and I noticed color rise up her chest.

"Good." Because she would be taking the rest of the night off. Now that I had her alone, there was no way I could take her back to that club tonight. I decided to change the subject. See if I could draw her out of her shell a bit. "So, what are you going to do with yourself once you are free, Sera?"

"Live my life," she told without hesitation. "The life I choose. Not one that's chosen for me."

"Is that how you see me?" I asked her. "Just another man telling you what to do?"

"Yes," she said. "And no. You did give me a choice to accept your offer or not."

"I did," I agreed. "However, you must know that even if you had said no, this would be happening between us anyway."

CHAPTER 15

Serafina

I glanced up at him, and then away, taking a sip of my drink as I tried to hide from the intensity of his stare. I could feel it, even though I couldn't see his eyes. But unless I wanted to crawl under the table or walk out of the room, there was nowhere for me to go.

With that thought, I suddenly stood up. I needed a moment.

Enzo's hand immediately wrapped around my wrist, keeping me there at the table. "Where the hell do you think you're going?"

"I just need to use the restroom," I told him as calmly as I could. But inside, I was freaking the fuck out.

He assessed me for a long moment. "Out the door and to your left, next to the kitchen." One finger at a time, he released me.

"I'll be right back," I told him.

Taking my coat to hide what I was wearing from the other patrons, I heard him say, "You have five minutes," right before I opened the door and walked out into the crowded restaurant. I scanned the room, but no one was paying any attention to me as I searched for the restroom sign and hurried in that direction.

When I got to the ladies' room, I shut myself in a stall and locked it firmly behind me, feeling like I could breathe for the first time since he'd shown up at the club. Jesus Christ and Holy Mother, what the hell had I gotten myself into? Even with his sunglasses, which he hadn't taken off once tonight, I could feel the heat of Enzo's eyes. They burned me everywhere they touched. He was always a bit...intense. But tonight, tonight was different. And I knew exactly why. He planned to keep me with him all night. That's why he'd told me to bring a change of clothes and why he was sticking to me like a bur. He wasn't going to give me a chance to get away. But even though I'd agreed to do this with him, now that the time had come, I didn't know if I was really ready for everything it entailed. I didn't know if I was ready for *him.*

I stared at the hearts written in permanent marker on the stall door, not really seeing them. I swallowed hard. This man was going to consume me until I didn't know who I was anymore. Until I didn't want to be anywhere without him. Until I *couldn't* leave him. And then he would discard me as men do. I'd seen it plenty of times. I'd watched as mafia men caught an interest in some unlucky woman. They would court them at dinners my father held. Pursue them like dogs after a bone until the woman was stupid enough to fall for their pretty words and possessive actions. And then once they had them, when the woman was so stupid in love with them they would do anything they said, the men would grow bored. They'd start yelling at them all the time. Calling them names. Breaking them down until the women were nothing but a shell of what they once were. And the men? They'd stop bringing their wives or girlfriends to the dinners and would show up with something new. Someone younger, prettier, but just as stupid. It made me sick to watch. I would not become one of those women.

Maybe I did just need to get out of this city. I had a little money saved, enough to get me to another state and set up for a month or two, but that was it. Not enough to have my name legally changed or to get a passport so I could leave the country, which was my ultimate goal. Somewhere where my father would never think to look, like Svalbard, that island way up by the north pole. He'd never think to look there. I hated the cold. He'd think I'd go somewhere tropical.

My phone buzzed in my jacket pocket. I pulled it out and checked the screen. There was a text from Enzo.

> You have two minutes and I'm coming in after you.

"Shit," I muttered to myself. Yanking down my ruffled panties, I quickly peed and washed my hands, then hurried back to the table. Our server followed me in with a tray.

"You just made it," he told me.

"What if I needed more time?" I asked, my face hot as I took off my coat and laid it back over my chair. "Thank you," I told our server as she set my plate on the table before me.

"Then you should tell me. Otherwise, I'm going to think you're trying to run off on me, Sera." He said it with a hint of a smile, but I knew he didn't find the thought funny at all.

"Can I get you anything else?" the server asked.

Enzo looked at me. I shook my head. "Thank you, I'm good."

She gave him a small bow. "I'll come check on you in a few minutes."

"Actually," Enzo stopped her before she could leave. "Would you mind giving us our privacy? I'll pay on our way out."

"Of course, Mr. Delligatti. No problem. Just crack open the door if you need anything and I'll come check on you."

"Thank you," he told her. Once she was gone, he took off his sunglasses and laid them on the table, then rubbed his eyes with his thumb and fingers of one hand. I watched him, noticing how strong his hands looked. Strength I already had personal knowledge of.

My heart was thundering in my chest, and I willed it to slow down. We were alone, but we were still in a crowded restaurant. He wouldn't try anything here.

Would he?

My pulse continued to race. I looked down at my food. It smelled delicious and my stomach growled in response, but I had no idea how I was supposed to eat. Picking up my fork, I put a small bite in my mouth, savoring the flavors. It was really good. And as Enzo dug into his dinner, I found myself beginning to relax.

We ate in an uncomfortable silence for a few minutes—at least on my part. Enzo appeared entirely at ease. I didn't look at him. I was afraid of what I would see without the shield of his glasses to block his emotions from me. But I could feel him watching me the entire time we ate.

When I was about halfway done with my meal and my stomach no longer grumbled in anger, Enzo set down his chopsticks and picked up his napkin to wipe his mouth. It hadn't escaped my notice that he had impeccable manners. "What's wrong, Sera?"

Surprised, my eyes flicked up to his before I could think to stop them. He was frowning, his brown eyes filled with genuine concern. It softened me a little to see that coming from him. I tried to muster up a smile for him, but I didn't think I was very successful. "Nothing. I'm fine."

"No. You're not. You're nervous. Did anything find its way into your pocket when you went to the restroom?"

I wasn't just nervous. I was terrified. I tried again for a smile, even as my face flamed with embarrassment. "No," I told him in answer to his question. "I'm just worried about what everyone will say when I get back to work."

His eyes roamed over my face, searching for the lie. But since that actually was one of the things bothering me, he appeared to believe me. However, I wasn't prepared for him to pull out his phone and call my boss again.

"It's me again. Sera won't be returning to work tonight. Please tell everyone she's ill, and make sure they believe you." Looking at me, he asked, "When are you scheduled to work again?"

"The day after tomorrow."

"She'll be back on Friday." Ending the call, he put the phone back in his jacket and picked up his chopsticks to resume his dinner.

I stared at him in disbelief. "I'm going to be so fired. Dammit, you can't keep doing that."

Raising his eyes to mine, he told me, "You're lucky I'm allowing you to keep the job at all."

Taken aback, I wasn't quite sure what to say. But this conversation was doing nothing to assuage my earlier fears. I sat stiffly in my chair and stared down at the remainder of my dinner. I needed this job. I *wanted* this job. I felt like an adult for the first time in my fucking life.

With a loud sigh, he set down his utensils and pushed away his plate, setting his arms on the table and leaning toward me. "What did you think was going to happen here with us? Hmm? We have an agreement, Sera."

The words came out of my mouth before I could stop them. "I thought you would fuck me, not ruin my life."

"Baby girl, I haven't even begun to ruin your life yet."

His dark eyes burned into mine. I could only stare at him.

Taking a sip of his wine, he pushed back his chair. "Come here."

He sat there like the mafia king he was, hard and without a shred of mercy anywhere in his body, except for his eyes. There was something in his eyes. And it was that glimmer of emotion I saw there that propelled me out of my chair and into his lap. I felt something hard pressing against my ass, and I adjusted the way I was sitting to try to get into a more comfortable position.

"You keep doing that, baby, and I'm going to have you face down on that table with my cock in your ass before we have a chance to finish our meal."

I stilled immediately, clasping my hands in my lap and keeping my eyes down. I felt weird in this position. Partly like the child I was dressed up as, but also a woman. One he was obviously sexually attracted to. But I didn't know what to do or what he expected of me, so I just sat.

Enzo's chest was rising and falling heavily against my side. He slid his hand beneath my thighs, lifted me up, and turned me so my back was against his chest. He hung my legs over his, then spread his knees wide so my legs did the same. I hung onto the arms of the chair as I watched him lift the bottom of my dress until my black ruffled panties were on full display. His chin rested on my shoulder so he could watch too.

Holding my dress up with one hand, he slid his other hand over my pussy until I was gripped in his palm. My eyes kept darting to the door. "Someone might come in."

"They won't," he rumbled in my ear. "And I want to touch you. So fucking bad, Sera." His fingertips found my clit through my panties, and my hips bucked, trying to increase the pressure as a rush of pleasure shot through me. He moaned in my ear, making the little hairs rise on the back of my neck and chills crawl down my spine. Instinctively, I tried to pull his hand away, and I felt him shake his head. "No. Keep your hands where they were."

His hand stilled, and I slowly put mine back on the arms of the chair.

"Thank you," he murmured.

My head fell back against his shoulder as he pulled my panties to the side and exposed me to the cool air of the restaurant. I could hear the other diners talking and laughing as they clinked glasses and enjoyed their meals together. Smelled the food coming out of the kitchen. But all I felt was Enzo's fingers as they found my folds and slid between them. I was wet, and he moaned again when he felt it.

The hand that was holding my dress rose higher up my torso, cupping my breast. And when that wasn't enough for him, he slid inside the neckline and under my bra to cup my bare flesh. My nipple hardened and grew sensitive against his palm, and I gripped the arms of the chair tight as his fingers found my clit again. Tension low in my belly gripped me and then released, and I couldn't stop myself from moving with each rise and fall of pleasure.

"Sera..." My name was low and harsh on his lips as he ground his hips up into my ass. I felt him probing my entrance with one finger, sliding in just enough for my body to protest the invasion before he went back to my clit. My breath left me, and my heart pounded in my ears until I couldn't hear anything else. I hung onto the chair so hard I was afraid I would break something, and on and on Enzo played my body with perfect precision, bringing me right to the brink but never letting me go over the edge.

"See how you respond to me?" he whispered in my ear. "See how your body moves against me? Fucking hell, Sera."

I ground my ass down against his hard length and he gasped into the back of my neck, sending shivers down my spine again. His hands clamped down on me, holding me still against him.

"Do not push me." His voice was suddenly cold.

"I'm sorry," I whispered.

He held me like that for a long time, only the sounds of our heaving breaths breaking the silence in the room. I heard someone greet some new customers. Heard dishes clank against each other as a table was cleared.

And then, gradually, he eased his grip on me. I felt his lips on the side of my throat as I relaxed against him once more, burning my skin with sinful kisses. I moaned when he found me again, and I tried to hold still, but I couldn't. Not entirely. He teased my clit and my nipple as he moaned in my ear, telling me how good I felt. Telling me all of the things he wanted to do to me. He pushed a finger inside of me as he pinched my nipple and told me how tight I would be around his cock.

I whimpered with need as he filled my head with visions of all of the ways he would use my body. My orgasm climbed, hovering on the edge until my muscles trembled and his name was a plea on my lips.

"Come for me, Sera."

I did as he commanded, my entire body going stiff as pleasure so fierce it was nearly pain started in my womb and shot through my body before it exploded through me in shock waves of pleasure. Enzo's hand slammed down over my mouth and his teeth sank into the muscle between my neck and shoulder as my orgasm wracked through me so hard my eyes nearly rolled back into my head.

I felt two of his fingers sink into me as far as he could reach, just enough that it began to hurt. I'd never had anything inside of me except a tampon. "You're so fucking tight," he told me. "Even now. I'm about to come just thinking about being inside of you."

He continued to run his fingers through my folds, coating them with moisture. Then, as I watched, he stuck them in his mouth so he could taste me. It was shocking. It was erotic. And I couldn't turn my head and pull my eyes away from the sight of him sucking my orgasm from his fingers.

Pulling my panties back into place and adjusting my dress, he lifted my boneless body and turned me, so I once again sat across his hard thighs. I felt his erection digging into my hip, and had to stop myself from rubbing my body against him for fear he'd carry out his earlier threat.

Gently, he turned my face to his and pressed his lips against mine, forcing my mouth open with his tongue. I could taste myself as he plundered my mouth, forcing me to submit to him. He broke off the kiss just as quickly as he started it, pressing his forehead against mine. "We need to leave."

"Okay."

"Stay here and put on your coat while I pay the check." Picking up his sunglasses, he slid them back onto his face.

"Okay." He didn't ask me if I wanted to keep my leftovers or not, and I almost called after him to get me a to-go box, but he was out the door before I could. It was more out of habit than anything, though, because honestly, food was the last thing on my mind.

He came back just as I was buttoning up my coat. "Let's go."

I walked out of the room knowing that if I ever came back, I wouldn't be the same woman I was now.

CHAPTER 16

Enzo

It took every ounce of willpower I had not to throw Sera into the back of the SUV and take her right there in the fucking parking lot. I could still smell her on my fingers, and my cock was about to burst out of its skin. But instead, I gritted my teeth and drove her back to the hotel. I didn't want to rush this. And I wanted her alone where we wouldn't be interrupted.

As soon as we were inside, I closed the door and locked it. I wanted to throw her against the wall and fuck her until she screamed, but I could see she was nervous again, so I held myself in check. Barely.

Sera walked straight over to the windows and stared out at the lights of the city, a steel rod in her back, though she tried to appear at ease.

I glanced around the room, taking inventory of anything she might steal so I could retrieve it later. Speaking of which..."Where is my watch?"

"It's in my bag." But she made no move to get it, so I went over to the chair where I'd dropped it and dug around until I found it. I slid it into the pocket of my slacks. I'd just be taking it off again soon.

Looking back over her shoulder, she asked, "Is this where you live all the time? In a hotel, I mean?"

Taking off my coat, I tossed it onto the chair and set my sunglasses on the desk. "When I'm not on duty, yeah. And those times are few and far between, so it doesn't make sense to pay rent or a mortgage every month on a place I'll barely see and wouldn't be able to take care of." Also, I liked to move around. I didn't have an army of guards to watch my back, and it was better that way. Less obvious. But it also made me an open target. I helped her take off her coat, laying it over mine. "Would you like a drink? Some wine? Whiskey?"

"Whiskey would be great," she told me without taking her eyes from the view.

Before I walked away, I leaned toward her and inhaled. Coconut. And something on her skin that reminded me of tropical flowers. A lotion, maybe. She smelled like warmth and sunshine. Like she should be lying on a beach somewhere, listening to the ocean pound away at the shore and drinking something frozen with an umbrella in it. Pulling myself away, I went to make our drinks and brought hers over to her. "Here you go."

"Thank you." She still wouldn't look at me. Just took the glass from my hand and held it in front of her. After a moment, she took a sip. Then another.

I stood beside her, staring down at her perfect profile. Then I set my glass down on the desk and reached for her hair.

"What are you doing?"

"Taking out these stupid pigtails." I tugged on the elastic bands until her pink hair tumbled around her face and down over her shoulders. Running my fingers through the strands, I untangled the knots until it fell in soft, loose curls. The scent of her shampoo filled the space between us. "Why the pink?" It wasn't that I didn't like it. I did. It suited her. I was just curious why she'd chosen it.

"Because my father hates the color. Especially on me."

"I like the color on you."

She met my eyes in the reflection, and then quickly looked away. She didn't complain when I continued to run my fingers through her hair, just stood quietly, allowing me to do what I willed and taking sips of her drink every few seconds.

I wanted to feel those soft strands brushing my bare skin, and I'd given her enough time to accept what was going to happen tonight. Taking the glass from her, I set it on the desk beside mine. She became very still, but didn't protest as she watched me in the reflection with big eyes. Finding the zipper on the back of her silver dress, I pulled it down, slowly revealing the creamy skin beneath. Sliding my hands up her back and over her bra straps, I pushed it off her shoulders. "Don't do that," I told her when she tried to hold it up in the front.

"People will see," she protested.

"Let them," I ordered. I didn't tell her that these windows were reflective on the outside so no one could see in, even at night. I didn't say anything else, just waited to see if she would obey me.

Hands shaking so hard I could see them in the window, she lowered her arms and let the dress fall to the floor until she stood in nothing but her black bra, black ruffled panties, black over-the-knee-stockings, and heels. Her breasts rose and fell sharply with each anxious breath, and her hands fisted at her sides.

I unhooked her bra in the back and slid the straps off her shoulders and down her arms until it joined her dress pooled at her feet. Staring at our reflection in the window, I stepped into her and wrapped my arms her from behind, holding her to me. She fit against me perfectly in her heels, the top of her head coming to just beneath my jaw.

Her breasts were beautiful, fuller on the bottom with slightly upturned nipples, as if they were begging for my mouth. I covered them with my hands, hefting their weight and feeling her nipples pebble against my palm as I squeezed the supple flesh. Sera's eyes closed as she leaned back against me.

"Open your eyes, Sera. I want you to see me touching you."

She did as she was told, her eyes slightly dazed as they watched my hands on her. Her paler skin contrasted against my olive tones as I left one hand on her breast and slid the other down her soft stomach to the waistline of her panties. Sliding beneath the band, I found her with my fingers. "So soft," I whispered. "So wet. Shall I fuck you against this window for the whole world to see, Sera?"

She shook her head.

"No? Why not?"

"Because I don't want them to see."

"Why not? You're mine now. Everyone should know that."

She sucked in a breath as I found the hard little nub hidden between the sweet folds of her pussy. "Because it should be something private."

"What? Us having sex? Or your naked body?"

"Both."

I buried my nose in her hair and closed my eyes, listening as her breaths became shorter, punctuated by soft moans. Despite her protests, her hands dug into my thighs, and she pressed herself against my fingers, much as she had at the restaurant. This time, I cupped her in my palm and ground the heel of my hand against her clit as I slid the tip of my middle finger inside of her sweet body. "So fucking tight," I murmured into her hair. A fresh surge of blood hardened my cock at the thought of sliding into that wet heat.

My self-control was hanging by a thread as I pushed her ruffled panties down over her hips and thighs until they fell at her feet. Then I straightened and stared at the picture of perfection before me.

She was a goddess born onto this earth to drive us mortal men to our knees. Soft and curvy, with that perfect face, an elegant neck, luscious breasts and hips that were made for a man to hang onto as he drove his cock into her tight pussy. Her legs were perfectly formed and sexy as all hell in heels and stockings. But she was right. This was not something I wanted anyone else to see.

With a possessive growl, I lifted her in my arms and carried her into the bedroom, where I laid her carefully on the white comforter. Light from the living room came through the open bedroom door. Enough that I could see her clearly. And my eyes never left her as I removed my tie and unbuttoned my shirt, ripping it from my shoulders. Kicking off my shoes, my hands went to the waistband of my slacks.

The entire time I undressed, Sera's wide eyes wandered over my body, searing my skin everywhere they touched. My nostrils flared as I watched her rub her legs together, seeking relief, and fisting the bed cover in her hands when she couldn't find it.

I slowed down when the only thing left was my boxer briefs, debated leaving them on in a vain effort to control myself just a little bit longer, and then decided it was a lost cause and kicked them off.

Grabbing Sera by the ankles, I pulled her to the end of the bed and removed her heels before rolling down each stocking in turn. Jesus, even her feet were pretty. Her toes painted a dusky pink to match her hair.

When there was nothing left to come between us, I started at the arch of her foot and licked and kissed my way up one leg. She tried to block me by keeping them pressed together, but it was way too late for that. "Open your legs, Sera."

"Enzo, please..."

"OPEN THEM." Lifting my head, I stared her down until she did as I asked, letting her knees drop open. "Thank you." My eyes traveled over her body and I lowered my head to continue what I was doing...

What the fuck??

The inside of one of Sera's thighs was bruised and cut. Even in the low light, I could see it was the shape of a hand, like someone had grabbed her from the back and dug his nails into the soft flesh just under her pussy. My vision blurred and my head roared as red-hot rage tore through my veins. My entire body began to tremble with the force of it. "Who did this to you?" My voice was low and rough with the effort it took to keep my anger under control. "Did this happen at your job?"

She tried to close her legs and sit up. To hide. But I wouldn't let her. "It's nothing."

I straightened to my full height and lifted her leg so I could see better in the light from the other room. Jesus fuck. Her delicate skin was blue and purple in a near perfect imprint of a hand. "Who the fuck did this to you, Sera? Was this someone at the club?"

"I'm not going to tell you," she said calmly. "So, please just let it go."

Let it go? Let it fucking go? Some *dead man* dared—DARED—to lay his fucking hands on her and she wanted me to let it go? "You can't ask me to just let it fucking go, Sera."

Anything else I was about to say was cut off when she reached down and slid her fingers between the folds of her pussy. Arching her back, she closed her eyes and wet her lips with the tip of her tongue before they parted on a moan.

The fury in my veins didn't leave, but it swiftly refocused on the sight of Sera writhing on the bed as she touched herself. She didn't want to tell me? That was fine. I had my suspicions. And tomorrow I'd have the tapes from the security cameras sent to me. I didn't know why she was protecting him, but it wouldn't keep me from finding out who the fuck had done this to her.

Pushing her legs as wide as they would go, I fell to my knees beside the bed and yanked her down to the edge. I ran my tongue from her ass to her clit, and that was where I stayed, wrapping my arms around her thighs and holding her against my mouth when she tried to push me away.

I worked her with my tongue until she cried out with the need to come. Until her heels dug into the mattress and I could feel her entire body tense. Pulling my mouth away, I kissed the soft flesh inside her thighs, seeing a flash of red when I saw the bruises again, then ran my mouth up over her hip as I moved her further up on the mattress. Grabbing her hips, I flipped her onto her stomach and pulled her up onto her hands and knees.

"Enzo..."

"Shhh..." Kneading her ass, I tongued her entrance, tasting the moisture there, then I rolled over onto my back with my face between her legs and pulled her down to my mouth.

"Oh, god..." She rocked back and forth on her hands and knees, taking her pleasure from my mouth. I wanted to fist my cock, but I was afraid if I touched myself, I'd come before I ever got inside of her.

But when she tensed over me and cried out, I couldn't take anymore. With one last taste that sent her over the edge, I dug my fingers into her hips and pulled her down my body until she was straddling my hips. Holding the base of my cock, I found her entrance and lifted my hips. She was so fucking tight I could barely get the head in. Out of my mind with lust, I acted more on animal instinct than anything else as I got a grip on her other hip and sat her down onto my stiff cock, filling her with one hard thrust.

My ears barely registered her scream of pain.

I almost didn't notice the way her entire body stiffened and her nails dug into my chest.

And then she tried to shove me away.

I bared my teeth, my cock pulsing with need as her body hugged it tight. Too tight. Holding her where she was with my hands on her thighs, I looked up into her perfect face, unable to contain the shock on mine. "Hold still!"

Tears streaked down her cheeks, taking a lot of her black makeup with them. Her expression was filled with shock and pain as she stared down at me with eyes that were too big for her face.

And fear. There was fear there as well.

Jesus Christ. She was a fucking virgin.

I didn't know why it had never occurred to me before now that she would be innocent. I'd just assumed that since she'd gone to college and worked in the club that somewhere in there, she would've had sex by now. Hell, she'd come to my door as an escort, for fuck's sake! For what? So I could do *this?*

"Fucking hell, Sera." But even as shock filled me, a primal feeling of possession crashed over me so hard I nearly growled like a beast.

"I was trying to tell you," she whispered through her tears, as though she was afraid of what I might do.

Still inside of her, I sat up and rolled her beneath me. She winced with the movement. "Shhh..." I moved her hair off her face. "Just give it a moment. The pain will fade."

A virgin. She was a *fucking* virgin.

I was the only man who'd ever been inside of her. Ever. And now she was truly MINE. And only mine.

Carefully, she moved beneath me as I brushed away her tears with my thumbs, then pressed my lips to hers. I felt her mouth tremble as I kissed her, slowly at first, and then with more urgency, sinking my tongue into the sweet warmth of her mouth. She tasted like innocence and fine whiskey. My muscles were fucking shaking with the effort it took for me to hold still and not drive into her like a man possessed as I kissed my way along her jaw, to her earlobe, and then down her neck to the sensitive spot between her neck and shoulder.

I pulled out until only the head of my cock was still inside of her and felt her stiffen beneath me, but I couldn't wait anymore. I needed to come. And I needed to be inside of her when I did it.

She began to cry as I sank back into her. Sweat dripped down my temples and my body screamed with need. "I'm so sorry, baby," I whispered, and then I gave in to my body's needs. Though my chest ached to cause her any amount of pain, I slammed into her over and over, her sobs in my ears and her body unyielding beneath me until I felt my balls tighten and I came deep inside of her, my entire body jerking with the force of it.

Afterward, I held her as she wept, murmured apologies and promises falling from my lips as I kissed her face. When I could breathe again, I carefully pulled out of her and sat back on my heels.

She laid spread out before me like a sacrifice, blood and come leaking out of her pussy. Pushing her knees wide, I leaned over and pressed a kiss to the bruised skin of her inner thigh, the scent of sex filling my nose. With my thumb, I caught the trickle of come and pushed it back inside of her where her body would absorb it—absorb me. "This belongs to me now," I told her. "YOU belong to me now."

And whoever hurt her would soon be praying for their death. A death I would prolong as long as possible.

CHAPTER 17

Serafina

I knew there would be some pain the first time I had sex. I knew because I'd read about it. And because I'd snuck a vibrator into my room once. A college classmate who I'd gotten to be friends with had snuck one to me when she found out I'd never been with a boy. But when I tried to use it, I'd been so nervous, and it had hurt so much I'd finally given up and hid the damn thing deep in my closet. So yes, I knew losing my virginity would hurt, but I never thought it would hurt like that.

However, it wasn't just the physical pain I cried from. It was the shock that he would do what he did, knowing it hurt me, like he didn't even care.

Clenching my teeth to keep my jaw from quivering, I closed my eyes tight, fighting back tears as Enzo ran his fingers up the crack of my ass to my pussy, collecting the remnants of his ejaculation and pushing it back inside of me. He hadn't worn a condom, and although I was on birth control to regulate my periods, I never thought to ask him if he was clean. I was stupid to think he would be considerate enough to protect me. "You didn't wear a condom." I couldn't keep the accusation from my voice.

"No," was all he said.

I covered my face with my hands and tried to roll to my side so I could hide my naked body from his burning eyes. But he clamped his hands down on my legs, just above my knees, and held me spread out beneath him. His thumb rubbed the inside of my thigh, pressing gently on the bruise there until I winced.

"Who left these marks on you, Sera?"

Although he didn't raise his voice, I could hear the barely controlled rage he tried to contain within it. I dropped my hands and opened my eyes to find him studying my face as he waited for an answer. Seeing him there, kneeling between my legs like some kind of masculine god, I almost forgot about the soreness between my legs. But his dark eyes burned through me, searing me down to the bone as he waited for my answer. I blinked a few times before I could speak. "I'm not going to tell you. Ever. So please stop asking me."

"You need to tell me."

"Why?"

He didn't respond. But he didn't have to. The look on his face told me everything I needed to know. I finally relented enough to say, "It was just a guy at the club who drank too much. He doesn't deserve to be punished."

"He hurt you. He deserves everything I want to do to him."

This time, it was my turn to be silent. The guy was an ass, but he didn't deserve to die the horrible death I could see in Enzo's eyes. I pulled the edge of the comforter up over me, half expecting him to deny me even that small comfort. But he didn't. I was shaking, but not from the cold. I felt exposed. Vulnerable. And underneath it all, there was hurt that he'd caused me so much pain and didn't appear to care at all. He was too obsessed with finding out who had dared to touch his "property."

But I was not okay. He frowned and reached for me, then pulled me up into his arms as I tried to drag the comforter up with me. He lifted me easily onto his lap, my knees on either side of his legs. The position made my pussy throb with aftershocks of pain, and a whimper escaped my throat. "Shhh..." he soothed as he held me. "I am sorry, baby. I never wanted to hurt you like that."

"Then why did you?" My voice was muffled from the quilt I was trying to hide behind. Were all men this unfeeling when it came to sex? Taking what they wanted with no consideration for the person they were taking it from?

His chest rose and fell against mine as he took a deep breath, and I felt his hand on the back of my head, smoothing down my hair. "I just...I'm so sorry I hurt you. That wasn't my intention." He paused. "I lost control. And I can't promise you it won't happen again, but I can promise it won't hurt like that again."

The emotions I'd desperately been trying to quell burst forth on a pathetic sob.

"Hey now...hey." He pulled me up tighter against him. I gave up trying to hang onto the quilt and wrapped my arms around his neck and buried my face into his shoulder. It was fucked up, I know, seeking comfort from the very person who had caused me such anguish. But despite everything that had just happened, his arms felt good around me. I felt safe. And before he shoved his dick inside of me, he'd made me feel good. So fucking good. He hadn't known I'd never been with anyone before. Maybe there was no helping the rest of it, I continued to rationalize. Maybe it would've only made it worse if he'd gone slow. It was better to just do it and get it over with, like ripping off a Band-Aid. "It won't be like that next time?"

"No, baby. It won't ever hurt like that again."

He held me tight as I hid with my face buried between his neck and shoulder. When the throbbing pain began to subside to a fluttering twinge and my tears dwindled down to sniffles, Enzo lifted up onto his knees and backed off the bed, taking me with him. Not ready to give up my hiding spot just yet, I wrapped my legs around his waist and tightened my arms around his neck. His low moan of satisfaction and pleasure caused the muscles low in my stomach to tighten with need.

I felt him walking across the room, and then he was setting me down on the closed toilet seat in the ensuite bathroom.

"Let go, baby girl."

Reluctantly, I released my death grip on his neck and dropped my arms down to my sides. Keeping my head down, I wrapped one arm around my breasts and let my other arm fall to cover the dark curls between my legs.

"Uh uh. Don't do that." Sitting on his heels in front of me, Enzo took my hands in his and opened my arms. "Don't hide from me." With a finger under my chin, he gently lifted my face until I was forced to meet his eyes. As soon as I did, I was hit with so many emotions I couldn't help but veer back to try to lessen the impact. But he shook his head. "Don't try to push me away, Sera. Don't do that to me."

"I'm not doing anything," I whispered. "I just..." How to put into words all of the things I was feeling right now? And did I even want to?

"Just what?"

I glanced up at him and then looked away, unable to take the intensity behind his gaze right now. "I've never been with someone like this, and it has me a bit...shook."

He studied my face for a long moment. "Okay," he finally said. "I can understand that." Then he rose to his feet and walked over to the tub, turning on the water.

"What are you doing?" I asked stupidly.

"Running a bath."

"Why?"

He didn't respond, he just sat on the side of the tub, completely comfortable in his nudity, and tested the temperature of the water with his hand. When he was satisfied, he turned to face me, resting his elbows on his knees. Once again, I was struck by how utterly beautiful he was, in a terrifying kind of way, and I couldn't keep myself from running my eyes over him with hungry appreciation.

Enzo was a big guy, with lean strips of muscle running beneath his skin, but not so much that he looked off balance like a bodybuilder. No, Enzo was strong, but not from lifting weights. Or maybe not just from lifting. To my untrained eye, he was built like a fighter. Lean and hard, without an ounce of fat on him. His left pec, shoulder, and upper arm were covered in black tribal tattoos. On his upper right arm was a dragon done in a similar style. And following the "V" of his right hip were words written in Italian. And although I spoke a little of the language, I'd only caught a glimpse of them and couldn't make out what they said.

"Because I need you to relax, and I don't want you to be sore."

My face burned. "Oh." Which meant he would want to take me again, and soon. I forced myself to meet his eyes. "What if I don't want to do that again?"

One side of his mouth lifted in the closest thing to a smile I'd yet to see on him. "I think I'll be able to talk you into it."

I said nothing, lest he think that was what I wanted. I needed a little time to process. "This is all just so weird for me."

"I know," he told me, then he reached over and shut off the water. "But right now, we're just going to take a bath."

"We?"

Standing up, he held out his hand.

Mine was still shaking when I reached out to take it.

Enzo gripped my hand tight and pulled me up, then assisted me into the tub, waiting patiently as I eased myself down into the hot water. On his command, I scooted forward and wrapped my arms around my knees as he climbed in behind me, watching the water nearly slosh over the sides as he sat down with a long leg on either side of me.

"Come here." Large, warm hands gripped my shoulders and eased me down until my back was against his chest. His erection was hard against my ass, but he just sighed and wrapped his arms around me.

Gradually, I felt my tense muscles relax. I let my head fall back to rest on the front of his shoulder. His heart beat strong and steady against my back, and his breathing was even in my ear. We sat there in the quiet until my eyes began to close, the life-changing events of the evening beginning to catch up to me. But my mind was racing. "Are you going to tell my father where I am?"

"No."

"Never?"

"Not ever, Sera."

"Do you promise?" I asked sleepily.

"I promise," he swore. "You don't ever have to go back there." There was a fierceness in his tone that calmed my fears. I believed him. "You're mine now," he said softly. "Only mine, Sera. He would have to kill me before I allowed him to take you from me."

"Okay," I whispered. For the first time in a long time, my mind was at ease. Despite everything, I felt safe, far beyond the reach of my father. I took a shuddering breath, and felt his arms tighten around me. This part wasn't so bad.

"Okay," he repeated quietly. He paused. "How about we talk about why you showed up at my door as an escort when you were a virgin."

"That should be obvious."

"Let's pretend it's not."

"So you could do exactly what you did tonight."

"Why?"

"Because if I was no longer a virgin, I wouldn't be as valuable to my father."

"And if it wasn't me?"

"Then I would've found someone else to do the deed."

He was quiet then, but I felt him tense behind me. I wasn't sure why that made him so upset. We barely knew each other, despite the fact that we'd just had sex.

He inhaled and exhaled heavily, then he lifted my arms from the water and placed my hands on either side of the tub. "Keep these here." Once he knew I would do as he told me, his hands moved to my breasts. Cupping the weight of them in his palms, he lifted them from the water. My nipples immediately hardened in the cold air, and he ran the pads of his thumbs over them, sending a sensation of heat straight to my core. "I don't like the idea of anyone else seeing you like this." He squeezed my breasts. "I'm the only one who gets to do that from now on."

Again, I stayed quiet. He felt like a lit fuse beneath me, and I was afraid to say anything for fear of detonating the bomb currently wrapped around me in the bathtub.

I sucked in a quick breath when he tweaked both nipples between his fingers, then I watched, fascinated, as he squeezed both breasts until they overflowed his palms.

"Open your legs for me," he ordered, and there was a deep huskiness to his voice I recognized.

I kept my voice as quiet as his. "Enzo, please. I'm still sore."

"I know, baby. It's okay. I won't hurt you again. Open your legs for me."

Hesitantly, I allowed my bent knees to drop to the sides of the tub.

"Good girl."

He said it right in my ear, and I shivered. His mouth moved down to the side of my throat. He found the artery there and ran his tongue along it, slowly, like a vampire savoring his next meal, and I wondered if he could feel how hard my heart was beating. Soft, wet kisses traveled down my neck until he found the muscle between my neck and shoulder. He sank his teeth into me at the same time he pinched my nipples and I moaned, my hips lifting of their own accord.

Holding me still with his bite, one hand slid over my stomach and down between my legs. Instinctively, I tried to close them, but when I heard his low growl of displeasure, I froze, then allowed them to fall open again.

His long, thick fingers found my folds and slid between them. I closed my eyes and moaned when he found my clit, rolling it gently between his fingers. Simultaneously, he did the same with my nipple, his fingers gentle where I was sore and a little rougher where I wasn't, until I was gasping for air and the muscles low in my core were tightening with pleasure.

He released my shoulder and ran his tongue over the skin where his teeth had been embedded just to the point of pain, before kissing his way back up to my ear. "I want to fuck you again, Sera." To emphasize his words, he rolled his hips beneath me, sliding his cock along the crack of my ass.

A whimper escaped my throat, part fear and part desire as he played me like a fine instrument.

"I want to, but I really don't want to hurt you again." He sounded torn between what he knew was right and the needs of his body. "You're so fucking perfect." One hand still teasing my nipples, his fingers slid lower between my legs until one fingertip pressed inside of me.

I flinched. I couldn't help it. It still hurt.

"Shhhh," he soothed, pulling his finger out and finding my clit again.

My muscles tensed from the attempted invasion, and it took me a minute to relax enough to feel the pleasure again. But he was patient, touching me so perfectly I began to wonder if there was a book out there somewhere on how to seduce timid virgins. Soon, my hips were rising and falling with each wave of painful pleasure that tightened and released low in my womb. My hands were gripping the sides of the tub so hard my fingers were beginning to hurt. And my body was aching for more. More of his mouth. More of his touch. More of the dirty things he was saying softly in my ear.

Lifting up, I ran my ass down the length of his cock, causing water to slosh up over the sides of the tub. Enzo groaned, his fingers moving faster on my clit and his other hand tightening on my breast. I did it again, fascinated with the sounds he made even as the waves of pleasure grew closer and closer until I was teetering on the edge of another orgasm.

Suddenly, he stopped, and I cried out in frustration before I could stop myself. His hand cupped my pussy, one fingertip teasing my entrance as my clit throbbed with need. "Enzo, please!"

He moved his hand, finding the perfect spot unerringly, working me up until my legs were shaking and my pussy throbbed.

Then he stopped, and I moaned.

"Do you want to come?" His voice was dark.

"Yes," I whispered. "Please, Enzo."

"I'll let you come, baby. But I need to be inside of you when you do it." His fingers barely brushed my clit, but my hips jumped up like a snake bit my ass. Cupping my pussy again, he used his grip to lift me up higher on his body and I felt the head of his cock probing my ass. "This will be mine, too," he warned. "But not tonight."

He couldn't possibly mean...

My thought was cut off when the length of him slid between my folds and Enzo groaned like he was in pain.

"Enzo—"

"Shhh...I'll go easy."

He lifted me again, and I felt him use his fingers to push his cock into position. Slowly and carefully, he lowered me down. I bit my lip as he stretched my sore passage wide, not stopping until he was fully sheathed inside of me. "Jesus Christ, Sera." His breaths were fast and heavy.

He was so deep, I felt like he was touching the bottom of my stomach. This time, I didn't feel the sharp pinch of pain when he breached my virginity, but a milder burning pain all throughout. "Enzo, please. It hurts."

"It won't hurt for long, baby." Holding perfectly still inside of me, he found my clit again. I was so sensitive, he barely had to touch me and everything clenched tight. "I fucking felt that," he said between heavy breaths. "Do it again, baby."

The warm water and my own fluids kept me slick for him as he began to move his fingers faster and harder. His arm tightened around my chest as my hips began to move of their own accord, rocking back and forth in rhythm with the waves of pleasure deep inside of me. His name left my lips, still begging. Not for him to stop this time, but to finish what he started.

"That's it, baby. That's it." His words of encouragement were hot in my ear. "Come for me, Sera."

As if I was just waiting for his command, my womb tightened to the point of pain and then toppled me over the edge. I convulsed on his lap, unable to hold still, and heard his grunts in my ear as he slammed into me with short, hard thrusts. Once, twice, three times until the heel of his hand pressed down on my pussy, holding me still as his cock pulsed inside of me and I knew he was coming. He sank his teeth into my shoulder again as his big body shuddered beneath me.

Afterward, we sat like that for a long time, his cock still inside of me and still half hard. With lazy strokes, he learned the curves of my body, touching me everywhere he could reach until the water grew cold. Carefully, he lifted me off of him and then helped me stand up. We moved from the tub to the shower, and starting with my hair, he washed me with firm, gentle hands before scrubbing himself clean as I watched. I was swiftly losing my shyness about being naked around him. It was almost impossible to feel insecure around this man when he openly worshiped every single part of me with his hands and mouth and words.

When we finished, he put me in his bed and curled his big body around mine, holding me tightly to him even in sleep.

I lay awake for a long time, unsure of what to feel. Part of me felt safe and snug and protected. But the other part, the one that fought so hard to get free of my father, wanted to bolt from the room and catch the next plane to anywhere. Just as long as it was away from this man.

However, why did I have the gut feeling there wasn't anywhere I could go now where he wouldn't find me?

CHAPTER 18

Enzo

I woke up to my phone ringing on the nightstand. The first thing I saw when I opened my eyes was Sera's pink hair. Her head was on my chest and one smooth, curvy leg was thrown over mine beneath the sheet that had ridden down to my waist.

I tightened my arm around her and pulled her closer, enjoying the feel of her bare skin warming mine for a moment before reality intruded on us. She'd been restless much of the night, and I knew it was because she felt strange having another person in her bed, not to mention what happened before we'd gotten there. But she would grow used to me soon enough. And then she would grow to depend on me. And perhaps she would even start to care about me.

Another ring pierced the air. Trying not to move too much, I grabbed my phone off my nightstand with my free hand and looked at the caller ID. It was Luca. I answered the call. "Yes."

"My apologies, Enz. I know it's supposed to be your day off, but I need you to come to the house."

"Do I have time to shower?"

"Yeah. If you could be here by one." It wasn't a question.

I pulled my phone away from my ear and checked the time. I had three hours. "Of course." Sera stirred beside me, and I looked down to see her eyes fluttering open. I put my hand over her mouth and shook my head in warning.

She froze beside me, her eyes wide on my face.

"I'll be there," I told him. I didn't ask him what it was about. It didn't matter. If Luca needed me, I would come. Not only was it my job, but he was one of only two people—now three—that I gave a shit about.

I left my hand over Sera's mouth until I ended the call and set the phone back on the nightstand. Then I removed it and brushed her hair out of her eyes. "I have to go into work," I told her. "I'm sorry. I was hoping we'd have the day together."

"That's okay," she said, her voice carefully neutral, as though she were afraid to upset me. "I need to run some errands anyway. What time is it?"

Rolling over onto my side so I was facing her, I studied her face. "It's early. You have plenty of time. How are you today?"

"I'm fine." She tried for a smile.

"Be honest with me, Sera."

She stared at me a moment, and then she blurted, "I'm sore. And nervous. And scared. And I'm feeling a little bit...overwhelmed. And I'd really like to go home so I can process all of this. Perhaps with a bottle of some kind of strong alcohol."

Frowning, I latched onto the one part that didn't make any sense. "Why are you scared?"

This time, there was no hesitation when she answered me. "Because I feel like I made a deal with the devil, and you're pulling me down into your hell, and a part of me likes it here. And that's what scares me."

Was that what I was doing? She gave me honesty. The least I could do was give her the same. "I'm hoping that, in time, being with me will be a refuge for you, and not something you dread."

Propping herself up on one elbow, she looked down at me. "I never dreaded being here. Not exactly. I was just...nervous. I wasn't sure what to expect." At my disbelieving look, she said, "Well, I knew the mechanics of it, but that was all."

I rolled over onto my back so I could see her face more clearly. "You can't tell me that a woman who looks like you do has never had any kind of sexual encounter, even if you didn't actually fuck."

"How could I?"

"You went to school. That had to afford you *some* freedom."

"I still lived at home. I was allowed to go to classes, with a bodyguard, of course, and then I was to come directly home. I wasn't allowed to make friends, or hang out after class." A wistful expression crossed her beautiful face. In the harsh light of morning, she was still ethereal. I couldn't stop looking at her. "Although there was one girl who was my lab partner one semester who I talked to a lot. But I was never allowed to see her outside of class."

Her chest and face flushed as she told me about that girl. "Did you want to fuck her?"

"What? No. Not at all." She appeared genuinely shocked. "I'm not attracted to women that way. Not that there's anything with wrong with that," she was quick to add. Then she eyed me with curiosity. "Are you attracted to men?"

"No. Then why the embarrassment when you talk about her?"

She stared down at my chest and shrugged one shoulder. I got the impression she wanted to touch me, but she didn't. "I don't know." Her eyes flicked up to mine. "We would just talk about a lot of stuff."

"Like sex?"

"Mmm hmm." She nodded. "And she was very graphic in her explanations, that's all."

There was something else about this girl that she wasn't telling me about, but I decided not to press her. We had plenty of time for that. Right now, I wanted to fuck her again. "How sore are you?"

Something in my voice made her eyes fly to mine and grow wide. "Again? Now?"

I pulled the sheet down past my hips, enjoying the way the blood rushed to her face when she glanced down and saw my erection.

"Sera."

Her eyes met mine.

"Do you like the way it feels when I touch you?"

She hesitated only slightly. "Yes."

I nearly moaned with the way she said it. "Do you like it when I kiss you?"

"Yes."

"Do you trust me when I say it won't always hurt like it did last night when I fuck you? That the pain will go away?"

"I know," she said. "It wasn't as bad the second time in the tub." Her gorgeous eyes traveled down to my chest again.

"Do you want to touch me?"

"Yes," she breathed.

My cock jerked, and my breath left me in a rush. There was nothing I wanted more in this fucking world that to have her hands on me. Her mouth would be even better. I could see the curiosity in her eyes. "You can touch me whenever you want to. You don't have to ask."

She sucked her bottom lip into her mouth and bit down. "I don't want to do anything wrong."

"You won't." She was still hesitant, so I reached over and grabbed her hand and pressed it over my heart. It pounded so hard I felt lightheaded as I lay there waiting, the anticipation nearly fucking killing me.

I'd never been a patient man when it came to sex. I took what I wanted from the women I was with. It just so happened that one of the things I wanted was to watch them come for me, so it usually worked out well for both parties.

But right now, with Sera, I sensed I needed to let her do this. Although I knew she enjoyed the way I touched her, she needed to know she could trust me. And I was more than happy to let her explore. "Touch me, Sera. Do anything you want." Releasing her hand, I let my arm fall back down to the bed.

Her fingertips began to move, slowly at first, delicately tracing the lines of the tattoo that covered my left pec. With a quick glance at my face, she pushed herself up until she was sitting on her heels beside me, gloriously naked. Jesus Christ, I'd never get tired of looking at her.

I fisted my hands into the sheets and tried to control my breathing as her eyes traveled quickly over my face, then dropped to my shoulders, my chest, down my stomach...all the way to my cock jutting out from between my hips.

"You're fucking killing me here, baby girl." The words were punctuated by quick, hard breaths as I tried to hold myself still on the bed.

"I'm sorry," she whispered.

"Don't be sorry, just fucking touch me."

Finally, *finally*, she did. Using both hands, she started at my neck and ran them down over my collarbone, feeling the curve of muscle in my chest. One hand stayed there while the other traveled slowly down my stomach. I held my breath when she stopped, undecided. "Go ahead," I told her.

But instead of doing what I told her, she removed her hand from my stomach and bent over me. Her pink hair fell like a cotton candy curtain between us, obscuring my vision until I couldn't see what she was doing. But I felt it.

Fucking hell, I fucking felt it.

Something soft and wet and warm touched the tip of my cock, just for a second. I was so fucking wound up by this point that I hissed through my teeth.

Her head whipped around, and she stared up at me, her forehead creased with worry. "I'm sorry. I don't know what I'm doing."

Moving one hand to her smooth back, I pressed her back down. "Do it again." My voice was dark with lust, but there was nothing I could fucking do about that. It was all I could do not to come all over her face with that one tiny touch of her tongue. "Take me in your mouth."

The look she gave me was unsure, but she did as I told her. Again, I felt the tip of her tongue gently lap at the head of my cock. My legs moved restlessly beneath the sheets and a deep moan escaped my throat. She *was* trying to fucking kill me.

With little licks, she explored my sex, one hand braced on my stomach and the other finding its way to my thigh. I wished I could see what she was doing, but her face was turned away from me.

Then she parted her lips and sucked the entire head into her mouth. I cried out, my hips jerking up off the bed, trying to go deeper. She immediately pulled back and my frustration was so great I nearly pounded my fists into the mattress. "Sera..." Her name was wrenched from my throat.

I heard her breath catch and opened my eyes to find her staring at me with a newfound sense of power. But as she stared into my eyes, something she saw there drained the triumphant look from her face. "You don't like this."

I shook my head. "No, baby. I fucking love it. But I only have so much control. And if you don't take me in your mouth right fucking now, I'm going to have you on your back with my cock inside of you so fucking fast...and I don't want to do that. I want to take my time with you. I want to make you feel so good you're begging me to fuck you."

Her chest rose and fell with quick breaths.

"Suck me, Sera. As deep as you can."

Her fingernails dug into my chest, and then she leaned over me again, letting her hair fall so the soft strands brushed my lower stomach. Gathering it in my hands, I held it up on the back of her head so I could see.

Soft lips closed around me again. I moved all of her hair into one hand and grabbed the base of my cock, standing it up straight so she'd be forced to give me her profile. The sight of her mouth stretched around me combined with the way her wet, warm tongue was exploring had me trembling with the effort it took to hold myself still. "Deeper," I ordered gruffly.

Sera did as I told her, opening her mouth wider and sliding down my length. Her tongue licked me all around and then she came up, sucking hard before releasing me. "Yes," I hissed. "Just like that. Again," I demanded.

With my hand on the back of her head, I showed her what I liked, and she soon fell into a rhythm that had me grinding my teeth and lifting my hips to thrust. "I'm gonna come, baby. Fuck." My hand still wrapped in her hair, I held her still and quickened the pace. My balls tightened as white-hot pleasure shot down my spine and up the length of my cock. "Sera!" Her name was a hoarse cry as my cock pulsed and come shot into her mouth. I shoved her head down until I was as deep as I could go. Sera swallowed and moaned in the back of her throat, and I felt it all the way to my fucking bones.

Holy shit. I'd never come so hard in my fucking life.

And she took it all.

"Perfect, baby. So fucking perfect." I praised her as I smoothed her hair out of her face, hoping I hadn't hurt her, but damn. "Come here." Slipping my hands under her arms, I pulled her up my body until she was sprawled out on top of me. I ran my hands down her back and over the curves of her ass, digging my fingers into the supple flesh as I kissed her, tasting the saltiness of my orgasm on her tongue.

Flipping her onto her back, I kissed my way down her throat to her sweet breasts. "I just want to make you feel good," I whispered against her soft skin. "Let me make you feel good, baby."

Sera's moan was the sweetest response I'd ever fucking heard.

CHAPTER 19

Enzo

Two hours and forty minutes later, I was showered and dressed and walking into Luca's lake house after dropping Sera off at her car, her cries of release still echoing in my ears. Knowing that I was the only man who'd ever known her so intimately...it did something to me. Something I couldn't quite name.

I hadn't wanted to leave her, and I'd almost asked her to stay at the hotel and wait for me. But I didn't know how long I was going to be, and she had to work tomorrow. Besides, it would be good to give her a little time to heal so I could fuck her the way I wanted to.

I tried to get a read on her when I dropped her off, but she kept whatever she was feeling closed off tight, and it bothered me. Naturally, she still wasn't quite comfortable with our arrangement. That was to be expected. I was the first man she'd ever been with, and our situation was far removed from what girls dreamed their first time would be like. There was no courting. No flowers. No gifts. No getting to know each other.

When I'd offered the deal to her, I thought doing it this way would be the fastest way to get her out of my system. But instead, it had only ingrained her deeper into my psyche. The more I touched her, the more I wanted to touch her. The more I heard her voice, the more it soothed me. The more I was inside of her, the more I craved to be deep within her. Her pussy. Her mouth. It didn't matter. As long as we were physically connected.

Without her next to me, I felt cold and alone and could only think of being with her again. And that's what made this thing between us dangerous.

I ran my fingers through my hair, fighting myself. I craved this woman more than anyone I'd ever met before. Maybe even Alessandra. But I also knew that me coming into her life wasn't a good thing for her. Just like my wife, she was trying to get out of this life. And all I would do was drag her deeper into it.

"Hello, Enzo!" Lisa, Luca's housekeeper, greeted me as I passed by the kitchen. She was the only one allowed in the house besides Veda, Tristan, and I. Unlike a lot of mob bosses and underbosses, Luca kept his staff to a minimum. He didn't trust too many people having free rein inside of his home.

"How are you, beautiful?" I asked her.

But, as usual, my flirtatious words had no effect on her. She just rolled her eyes and said, "Luca and Tristan are already in Luca's office. Would you like some coffee or tea?"

"No, thank you. I'm good."

"Alright, I'll be in here starting dinner if you change your mind."

"Thank you." I gave her a nod and headed down the hall, where I could hear my two best friends talking. I walked in to find Luca behind his large desk looking over some papers and Tristan sitting on the couch in the sitting area in front of it. They both looked up when I walked in.

"Enzo, thank you for coming," Luca said.

I took off my sunglasses and tucked them inside of my suit coat. "Of course. What's going on?"

His face gave nothing away. "Tristan found our lost mafia princess."

My heart stopped completely, and then began to pound with slow, hard beats, making me lightheaded. "Ciro's daughter?"

"Yes," Tristan said. "She's here in Austin and working at a club downtown we protect. I believe it's the one Jade and the other escorts have made their unofficial place of work."

"It's very private," Luca added, "and I respect that, which is why it took Tristan a minute to find out she was an employee. You've been there, haven't you?" Luca asked me.

They both knew that I preferred to keep my dates professional, and that Jade had been my steady date for years, until now. "Yes. I met Jade there the first time I was introduced to her. They like to keep things public the first time, for safety reasons." I didn't bother to tell them of how I'd frequented the club since meeting Sera.

"The girl, Serafina, is working tomorrow night," Luca told me. "Tristan will be waiting for her when she gets off and he'll take her to my father's until he can contact *her* father and send someone to get her. His new whore can take care of the girl until she's back where she belongs."

His eyes never left my face the entire time he told me this. I wanted to scream and rage that she didn't belong with him. She belonged with me. But I said nothing. Instead, I just sat there, my eyes on the table in front of me as I nodded along as though I was listening, while the entire time my mind raced as I tried to think of a way to get somewhere alone so I could warn Sera and tell her to run and hole up somewhere until I could get to her.

"Enzo, I'll need you to cover Tris's duties tomorrow night while he's taking care of this situation."

Wishing like hell I'd left my sunglasses on, I schooled my features as best I could. "Why don't you send me after the girl instead?"

Luca stared straight at me, and I knew he saw the truth in my eyes. He shook his head. "A situation has come up with one of our shipments, and I need you to handle it. You're better with people than Tris is, anyway."

I didn't worry that Tristan would take offense at Luca's comment. We'd all known each other a long time, and what he'd said was true. Tristan interacted emotionally with very few people. Everyone else might as well be androids wandering the world disguised as humans. And that was what made him one of the deadliest people I knew.

"Luca, may I speak to you alone?"

"I don't think that's necessary."

He knew. It was probably written all over my face. And the fact that he wasn't willing to talk about it told me all I needed to know. There would be no leeway where Sera was concerned. He was sending her back to her father.

Except...

Why was he telling me all of this today? When I would have plenty of time to warn her?

He saw the exact moment I understood. I turned the conversation back to the shipment issue. "What do you need me to do?"

As Luca explained what was going on, I realized there was no way in hell I'd be able to get to Sera tonight. Even if I did manage to find out where she was staying. My only chance was to call and hope she had her damn phone on her.

That, or come clean with the two people I trusted with my life and force Luca to make a different decision.

I took a breath. Then another.

Fuck it.

Rising from my seat, I interrupted Luca. "I'm sorry," I told him. "But we can't turn Serafina back over to her father."

Luca sat back in his leather chair. "Why not?" he asked quietly.

"Because I already found her. And I'm not giving her up."

"Fuck, Enz." Tristan stared up at me like I'd lost my ever-loving mind.

But Luca's expression gave nothing away. "Enzo, you can't keep her."

"Why not? She's not a child. She's twenty-five. Old enough to make her own decisions."

"And did she decide she wanted to be with you?"

"Did Veda?" I shot back at him. "When you first brought her here?" He'd stolen Veda right out of her home—well, her sister's home—because he thought she was his brother's fiancé and he wanted to kill her in front of him out of revenge. Scrubbing my hand over my mouth, I reined in my temper. "I haven't kidnapped her, if that's what you're thinking. If I had, she wouldn't still be working in that club."

"Then how do you know her?" Luca asked.

"She's a friend of Jade's," I answered. I didn't bother telling him that she showed up at my door trying to whore herself out in a desperate attempt to lose her virginity. "I didn't know who she was at first. Not until you brought it to our attention. But by then it was too late."

"Enzo, we have to let her father know where she is."

"Why?" I demanded. "She doesn't want to go back there."

"Because if we don't, and he finds out she's here in my city, it could cause a lot of problems we really don't need right now. Please sit down," he added when I began to pace.

I returned to my seat in the chair across from Tristan. "What if we make him a deal?"

"Are you going to marry this girl?" he asked.

"No." My answer was swift and came before I'd even thought it through. But as soon as the word was out of my mouth, I knew it was the correct answer. I would never put another woman through what Alessandra went through because she was married to me. A mistress, you could hide away. I could visit her as often as I could, and I could keep her far away from this part of myself. A wife was expected to be a part of the "family," and as such, there would be no escape for her from this life.

"Then there is no deal we could make that he would accept, and you know it. I take it you've already fucked her."

It wasn't really a question, but I answered it anyway. "Yes."

"Was she a virgin?"

"Yes."

Luca exchanged looks with Tristan, and then he put his elbows on his desk and rubbed his forehead.

"I'm not going to hurt her."

"That's not what I'm worried about."

"Then what *are* you worried about, Luca?" My tone was bordering on disrespect, and I tried to get it under control. "Look," I told him. "I didn't mean for this to happen. She showed up at my door when Jade couldn't make it for the wedding reception. I didn't know who she was until you showed us the photos of her." And by then, she was already in my blood.

"It's not too late," he insisted.

"Yes, it is," I told him. "I'm not sending her back to her father." Before he could argue with me further, a thought occurred to me. "Have you already notified him that she's here in Austin?"

"No. I wanted to make sure we had her before I told him."

"Then there's no reason to do so."

"There is one," Luca said. "Luigi. My father knows she's here."

Son of a bitch.

CHAPTER 20

Serafina

I was just leaving Jade's apartment to go to work when the cell phone Enzo gave me buzzed in my bag. Opening the passenger's side door to my car, I set it on the seat and pulled out the phone.

> Do not go anywhere. Stay where you are and wait for me to contact you.

Frowning, I typed a response.

> I was just going into work. One of the girls called in.

His response was immediate.

> Sera, do as I say. I will explain as soon as I can.

A second text came in right after.

Tell me you understand.

Oh, I understood fine. But I still needed to go in. He would be angry with me, but I already told my boss I would be there. Besides, I wasn't completely stupid. Enzo had promised me enough money to start a brand-new life...when he was done with me. But what if something happened between now and then? What if he decided I wasn't worth it, or changed his mind for some other reason? What was I going to do then? March into his hotel room and demand my money? I almost laughed out loud. He was mafia. If he lost his infatuation with me, or I did something to offend him, he'd put a bullet through me without thinking twice about it and my body would disappear, never to be found again.

I dropped the phone back into my bag, closed the door, and walked around the front of the car to get into the driver's side. But instead of starting the engine, I just sat there for a minute, staring out the windshield.

Butterflies fluttered around inside my stomach and my heart pounded behind my ribcage. As cool as I tried to sound via text, the truth of the matter was I was very much affected by the thought of seeing Enzo again tonight. Last night had been hard. I'd spent most of it trying not to cry, and not just because of the physical pain of a man entering my body for the first time, but also because of the emotional rollercoaster I'd gone through. Emotions I hadn't been expecting and that I'd tried very hard to hide. It had all been so...overwhelming, to say the least. I'd almost hated him last night. And I'd almost hated myself for getting myself into this situation.

But this morning had actually been kind of...nice.

No. Nice wasn't the word. Mind blowing. Yeah, that was it.

My phone rang right as I started the car and was about to pull out of the parking lot. I put it back into park and rummaged around in my bag until I found my cell. "Hello?"

"Sera." Enzo's voice was hushed, but no less commanding.

"Yes?"

"Why didn't you answer my last text?"

"Because I'm in my car. I'm going to work." I kept my tone firm. I really needed to make up the time I missed last night because of him.

"You can't go into work, Sera. You've been found."

My heart stopped and my entire body went ice cold. "What?"

"My boss found out you're here in Austin. But don't panic. I talked to him and he's not going to turn you in just yet. However, your location has been leaked to the boss. We don't have very much time to get you somewhere safe. You need to lay low today until I figure something out."

It took me a moment to find my voice. "I appreciate that. But I'm not your problem, Enzo."

"Sera—"

"Goodbye, Enzo." I hung up the phone and shoved it back into my bag, ignoring it when it started ringing again, then I turned off the car and ran back upstairs.

It took me all of fifteen minutes to change into jeans, sneakers, and a T-shirt and hoodie (so I could hide my hair), and pack my clothes in a suitcase I took from Jade's closet. I left her a quick note, thanking her for letting me stay there and for everything she'd done for me. I didn't sign my name, or tell her I'd be in touch. Because it would be a lie. I couldn't risk any communication once I was gone.

I had cash hidden in a rip in the fabric underneath the couch. No one other than me knew it was there. Not even Jade. I pulled out the cloth tote bag and unrolled it. It looked like everything was there, so I rolled it back up and stuck it down into my suitcase.

Back in the car, I debated stopping by the club one last time to try to pick up the paycheck they owed me. It was the end of the pay period, and they actually paid pretty decent, so it would be a sizable chunk of change I'd be leaving if I just took off.

I ran through what Enzo had told me on the phone. If what he'd said was true, I should be okay to stop there one last time and let them know I was leaving and get the money they owed me.

Mind made up, I maneuvered my way out of the neighborhood and onto the highway, heading toward work.

When I got there, the club was just opening, and the back lot was already pretty full of vehicles owned by the other employees. I pulled into my parking spot, got out of the car, and locked it with my key fob as I hurried toward the back door. The guard assigned to me wasn't there, but I was filling in for someone else and it wasn't on the schedule. He probably didn't know I was coming in.

"Why aren't you dressed for work?"

I nearly screamed as I spun around, my heart pounding out of my chest. It slowed down when I saw a man in a suit standing beside a slick, black BMW sedan, then it sped up again as he stepped into the light of a lamppost. It was the guy who couldn't keep his hands to himself. The one who'd left bruises on my inner thigh. "I was just heading in to change," I told him. I didn't smile this time. "I'll see you inside."

"Then where are your clothes, baby doll?"

I kept walking, calling back over my shoulder, "Inside." I didn't know what he was doing in the back lot. It was small and for employees only. My instincts were telling me to get away, and to do it as fast as I could.

I was three cars away when he grabbed me. One hand covered my mouth and nose as his other arm wrapped around my middle, pinning my arms down to my sides as he hauled me back against him.

"You think you're too good for me?" he said in my ear. I couldn't breathe, and I fought against his hold, trying to pull his hand off of my face, but the dude was freakishly strong. "You're not, you know. I can buy any woman in this place, baby doll. You're not fucking special."

The entire time he talked, he was dragging me backward into the lot. I kept my eyes glued to the back door, praying someone would come out. I tried to scream, but it was muffled by his large hand. I started to see spots and knew I didn't have much time.

I heard car locks beep and a latch open, and then he was shoving me into the trunk of the BMW. As soon as he let go of me, I sucked in a lungful of air and screamed as loud as I could as I threw myself toward the opening, but he knocked me back with a hard backfist across my face. I hit my head on the car as I fell back, and for a moment, everything went black around me.

"You're not too good for me, bitch. And I think you need to be brought down a peg or two."

The trunk slammed shut, and I was alone in the darkness. I heard the car door slam and the engine start. Frantically I searched for the emergency release that every new car had just in case a child—or an adult—got stuck in the trunk. I found a hole where it should be, but there was no cord to pull. Then I rolled over and started feeling around the back seats, but I couldn't get them to budge from my position inside the trunk.

Even knowing it wasn't there, I searched my pockets for my cell phone as I tried not to panic. But of course, I couldn't find it. It was back in my bag, sitting on the front seat of my car.

As the screams rose inside of me and horror turned my blood to ice, I let the panic take over, kicking and banging my fists against the trunk, praying someone would hear me, and knowing it was too late.

CHAPTER 21

Enzo

I slammed my fist into the side of the delivery truck that was supposed to be full of Luca's product. Then I hit it again. And again. Until blood smeared the dirty white surface. But I didn't feel the pain.

Gripping my phone in my left hand, I tried to call Sera *again*. And then again.

"Goddammit, baby. Where the fuck are you?" I swung around, my eyes skittering wildly from side to side behind my sunglasses without really seeing anything. "Think...just think...where would she go?"

If anyone could see me right now, they'd think I'd lost my fucking mind. And they wouldn't be entirely wrong. But this truck had been abandoned on a lonely strip of highway halfway between Austin and Mexico, the pounds of meth it was transporting gone. And I was still waiting for some of Luca's soldiers to arrive and drive it the remainder of the trip, where we would hide it in one of our warehouses until we could figure out what the hell happened.

In the meantime, I was stuck here while Sera was...who the fuck knew where.

Taking a deep breath, I forced myself to calm down. If she had her phone on her, even though she wasn't answering it, I could get a location on her. I pulled up the tracking app I'd installed on her phone before I gave it to her and saw her photo in downtown Austin.

The club. Of course! If they owed her money, she would make an appearance there. I called the guard I'd hired to watch over her. "Have you seen Sera?" I nearly shouted into the phone when he answered.

"I was just about to call you," he responded. "Her car is here, but no, I haven't seen her."

"She didn't come into the club?"

"No, sir. I was alerted by the manager that she was coming in tonight and I was waiting outside for her like I always do. When she didn't show up after about twenty minutes, I went inside to check to see if something had been changed. It wasn't. So I walked out into the club proper to see if maybe she'd gotten a ride or come in a different way or whatever. The bartender told me she'd never shown up. When I went back outside, her car was there. Sera was not. The vehicle is locked, and her bag is inside on the passenger seat."

I couldn't breathe. I couldn't fucking breathe.

"Mr. Delligatti? Sir?"

"You saw *nothing*," I reiterated, even though he'd just said he hadn't. "You have no idea if she got into a car willingly with someone."

"No, sir. I'm waiting for the manager to arrive so he can pull up the security feed for the back lot."

"Thank you. I'll be there as soon as I can." Ending the call, I immediately called Luca. "How far away is your driver?"

"About forty minutes. Why?"

"Did you send Tristan after Sera?"

The accusation wasn't missed. There was a slight pause. "No, Enzo. Tristan is sitting right in front of me. What's happened?"

"Fuck...FUCK!" I looked around, searching for answers along the side of the abandoned highway. My gut clenched, and I couldn't seem to get enough air.

"Enzo! What's going on with Sera?"

I took a few deep breaths. "She's gone," I told him. "Her car is parked at the club where she works, but she never came inside. I have to go. I can't fucking wait around here."

"Just wait a minute. Stop and think. Would she have gone off with someone?"

I shook my head. "No. I think she went there to pick up her paycheck."

He was silent for a long time. "What?" I finally asked him. But I didn't have to ask. I knew what he was thinking.

"Enzo, it's likely her father found out she was here in Austin and sent someone to get her."

"Is there a way you could find out without giving her away?" My jaw was clenched so hard I could barely get the words out.

"Give me five minutes." He hung up the phone.

As I waited, I paced, concentrating on my breathing and counting my steps. I didn't have time for a full-blown panic attack. When the phone rang, I closed my eyes and lifted it to my ear.

"It wasn't her father. He's still searching for her."

"Luigi?"

"No. My father is preparing for a trip and told me to handle it."

An ugly feeling began to creep through my insides. "I have to get to the club, Luca."

"Is the truck clear?"

"Yes. The key was still in the ignition and there's nothing that will lead anyone back to you. I checked it twice when I first got here."

"I'll meet you at the club." He hung up the call.

Even though I wanted nothing more than to tear out of there, I pulled gloves onto my shaking hands and went through the cab of the truck one more time, then checked underneath and all around before opening the back and doing one last sweep. It was completely clean. Jumping out, I closed the back, locked the doors, and buried the key. Then I texted Luca to let him know where it was so he could tell his driver and got into my car.

I made it back to Austin in record time. Luca was already there when I arrived. He was in the office with the manager, going through the video feed of the back entrance, each in front of a different monitor on the desk. Sera's guard stood by the door. "Have you found anything?"

"Yes. Just now." He pointed at the monitor in front of him. "Do you know who this guy is?"

Taking off my sunglasses, I leaned down beside Luca until I was eye level with the guy's face. Luca glanced at my bloody knuckles, but said nothing.

Sera was talking to a man in the back parking lot. I knew it was her even though I couldn't see her face and she had the hood of her sweatshirt pulled up to cover her hair. And by the way she held herself, I could tell she was uncomfortable.

No, not just uncomfortable. She was afraid.

An ice-cold calm filled me. Screaming and punching things, although it might make me feel better, would not get Sera back. Neither would panicking.

I was so focused on her that I almost missed the face shot of the guy she was talking to when he turned his head slightly to follow her movements as she tried to walk into the club. Then he looked straight up into the camera, and we lost the picture. When it came back, he and Sera were gone. And so was the car he stood near. Hers was still in the lot. "Back it up," I ordered the manager.

He did, and I watched it again. "Can you zoom in on that plate number?"

"I'll try," he told me. "But I don't know how close I'll be able to get before it goes blurry."

"Do the best you can."

"You know him?" Luca asked me.

"Yes. That's Derek Jonak. He's a customer who's been harassing her." It all clicked together the moment I saw him waiting for her. "He was bothering her one night when I was here. One of the other waitresses gave me his name, and I pulled up some info on him. He's a business guy. Runs a tech company. Thinks he's hot shit and above everyone else. He left bruises on the inside of her thigh. A few nights ago, I believe, when I wasn't here."

"Apparently, he has a thing for your girl."

"Looks that way," I murmured as I wrote down the plate number. "Let me have the computer."

Luca ordered the club manager out of the way and gave me his chair. "As soon as you know anything, I'll call in some guys. I need two to stay with Veda, but the rest are all yours."

"I won't need them," I told him. "I can handle this myself. But thank you."

"Enzo, you don't know what you're walking into."

"It doesn't matter," I told him as I went incognito and typed in a website. "I let this happen to her, and I'll get her back."

A few minutes and one phone call to Tristan later, and I had a general direction of where he was headed with my girl. Although traffic cameras weren't always our friends, they did come in handy at times like these.

"Enzo." Luca stopped me from leaving with a hand on my arm. "Are you sure you don't want me to come with you? Or a few of the men?"

"No. This son of a bitch is mine. I'll call you when I have her."

"Check in with me before then and keep me updated, alright?"

I nodded and walked out of the office and out of the club, checking the clip in my gun before sliding it back into its shoulder holster. In the SUV, I opened the glove box and pulled out the backup weapon I'd taken with me to the abandoned truck. I also had a knife strapped to my right calf. If I had my way about it, I wouldn't be needing any of these weapons. I'd rather kill him with my bare hands.

This motherfucker would not be leaving our meeting alive.

With Tristan coming over the Bluetooth, we tracked the bastard. He was heading south toward San Antonio, and I broke out into a cold sweat with every mile that went by. There were reasons women were taken to San Antonio, and none of them were good.

We lost him when he hit the city limits, and I pulled over at a gas station. He had a good three hour start on me, but there was no sense in driving around aimlessly when I had no fucking idea where he went.

I fought down the feelings of panic that threatened to overwhelm me.

"Enzo? You still there?" Tristan's voice came over the car's Bluetooth.

"I'm here."

"Where's here?"

"I pulled over at a gas station just inside San Antonio." My sunglasses sat beside me on the seat, and I rubbed my eyes with the thumb and forefinger of my right hand. "She can't be gone, Tris." I said it so quietly, I didn't know if he heard me.

"She's not," he told me. "We'll find her. Stay where you are and let me make a few phone calls."

"Thank you." I ended the call and shut off the car. Tristan was calling his contacts in the area and putting out the word that we were looking for the high-tech mogul who'd taken my girl. If he was smart, which he must be to have gotten where he was in the world, he would've changed cars somewhere along the way. However, he was also way too cocky and probably thought he could get away with whatever the hell he wanted to. So, the chances were about fifty-fifty he was still in the same vehicle.

While I waited, I checked my weapons again just to give myself something to do, my mind replaying Sera the way I'd last seen her just that morning. She'd smiled at me just before she got out of the SUV. It was timid, but it had been real, and it'd made my heart race.

I wondered if I'd ever have the chance to get to know her the way I wanted to. Or get to lavish her with gifts. I wanted to talk to her about stupid shit like what television show was better, and serious stuff like what her life was like as a young girl growing up with her father. I wondered if she'd ever been in love, and then had to stop thinking about that because it made me want to rip apart the unknown boy she may or may not have known.

I wondered if she'd ever accept being with me, or if it would be a constant battle when I told her I wasn't giving her up.

My cell rang as I was watching a couple of underage kids try to get someone to buy them something they couldn't buy themselves. Probably beer. "What did you find out?"

"Derek Jonak's car was spotted on a dead-end road in Wheatley Heights two hours ago."

I closed my eyes. "Motherfucker." Bad things went on in that east side neighborhood. "Do you have an address?"

Tristan gave it to me, along with the information that the car was no longer there. I punched it into my GPS, thanked him for his help, and hung up.

It took me another twenty-seven minutes to get to the east side with traffic. I drove by the house first, turned around in the circle at the end of the road and parked across the street facing out toward the main road. The house was one-story, with dirty yellow siding and thick curtains across the windows. I could see another window toward the back that had bars. The house was completely dark, and there were no vehicles in the drive.

Sliding my sunglasses onto my face, I got out of the SUV, leaving it unlocked. I wouldn't be here long. As I walked up to the front door, I unbuttoned my coat, so I'd have easy access to my weapon. I gave the door a casual knock and listened.

No one answered, and I didn't hear any footsteps.

With a quick look up and down the street, I took two steps back and gave the front door a strong kick. Two more and I was inside, the doorframe hanging loose where the rotting wood had been ripped through by the lock. I pressed up against the wall and pulled out my gun.

Again, I listened, but there was only silence.

Feeling for a light switch, I flipped it on and the living area I stood in was flooded with light. It was empty except for an upside-down bucket and an empty Dos Equis box. Kicking the door closed behind me, I began to make my way through the house room by room, flicking on lights as I went. Adrenaline raced through my veins, sharpening my senses as I crept quietly across the floor. I kept my gun aimed directly in front of me, even though I had no intention of shooting anyone unless I had to. No. I wanted to smash in faces. Rip out intestines. Tear apart any motherfucker stupid enough to mess with what was mine.

But all I found were more empty rooms.

Letting my arms fall to my side, I kept my weapon palmed just in case, and walked into the back bedroom.

The one that had the bars on the windows. There was a bare mattress on the floor with a dirty pillow and no blankets. I began to leave, but stopped. Something propelled me across the room. I stared down at that mattress, then bent over and picked up the pillow. Bringing it to my face, I inhaled.

The scent of coconuts and tropical flowers hit my nose.

Pain slammed through the middle of the chest, and I hugged the filthy thing to me for a second, telling myself this was good. It meant she was still alive.

I don't know how long I stood there holding that pillow, but when I was able, I dropped it back onto the mattress and called Tristan.

"What did you find?"

"An empty house. But she was here, Tris."

He didn't ask me how I knew. "That's good."

"I need to know who owns this house and what they use it for. There's no furniture other than a mattress in the back bedroom, which is barred, so no one can get out unless they go out the front door. It's not someone's home. It's a drop-off point."

"I'm on it." He paused. "This might take a while, Enz. Why don't you come back to the lake house?"

He was right. There was no use staying here. I had no idea where Sera was now or where they could've taken her. All I'd be doing by staying here was making myself a target. "I'm on my way."

Hang on, baby girl. I'm coming to get you.

Keep reading with His Rejection.

ABOUT THE AUTHOR

Hi! My name is Angel Rayne and I write dark, delicious romance with antiheroes who would burn down the world to save the woman they love. I never understood why the villains never win the girl, and so I decided to write them their own love stories where they do.

 Here are a few other odds and ends about me...

-Music inspires my stories and I make playlists for every book.

-I am not a fast writer. My stories take time to write. They need to brew in my head. To have book releases close together I have to write ahead. But I would much rather take the time the stories need to be the best they can be than try to rush them out. Trust me on this one.

-I love the rain, and I'm happiest when I'm sitting in a coffee shop with my laptop as it storms outside.

-I prefer to go watch movies alone, with one of those fancy coffees hidden in my purse. (Yes, I really do this.)

-My husband calls me his "little bird" because anything that sparkles catches my eye.

-I will never have enough soft blankets. Ever.

-I love ALL THE DRAMA...but only in books.

-I will forever re-watch The Phantom of the Opera with the hope that by some miracle, this time Christine will choose the right guy.

Thank you for reading my stories, and I always love to hear from you! You can reach me at: angel@angelrayne.com